The scent of the lilies

T.S. RILEY

For further information, write
toddsriley@gmail.com

9798218406738 ISBN E-Book
9798218406721 ISBN Print

This is a work of fiction.
Names, characters, business, events and incidents
are the products of the author's imagination.
Any resemblance to actual persons, living or dead,
or actual events is purely coincidental.

I dedicate this book
to my husband, Aindréas,
who has always encouraged me
to chase my dreams.
And to all those
who have been forced
into the shadows
by your own bullies,
I see you.

1

IMARI

I used to come to this pond all the time as a child with my mom. It is perfectly hidden at the end of a long trail in the woods across the street from our house. You could miss the entrance to the path so easily if you didn't know where to look. The key was to locate the old dogwood tree—completely out of place amongst the Georgia pines. Behind that tree, through overgrown bushes that you had to move out of the way, was the start of the trail. As you stepped into the trail, the woods opened up like a hidden world. Mom would tell me that these woods had been here for hundreds of years, back when this neighborhood was used for sharecropping. She said some of these trees were alive all the way back then.

"We can learn so many great lessons from these

trees, Imari," she'd said. "Their roots are all inter-connected. They understand each other. They are all fighting for the light and, sometimes, in their pursuit of it, they block out another tree's chance at the sun. But those trees that are persistent, who insist on never giving up, they push their way through the other trees—taking up space in these woods—space they believe they deserve. You may also need to fight for the light in your own life someday, little one."

I had not known then what she meant but I loved the way she saw the world. She was always taking what seemed like a normal environment and adding color to it. It opened my mind to so many possibilities.

My mom had the best imagination. She would tell me stories of princes and princesses on magical jour-neys as we would navigate along the path. I would imagine myself on those adventures, but I could nev-er really decide: did I want to be the one saving or did I want to be saved?

At the end of the path was this pond, tranquil and surrounded by lilies. My mother described the scent of the lilies as the smell of a newborn baby, the sweetness of the first bite of a perfectly ripe peach dripping at the corners of your mouth. She loved to sit along the pond's edge and feed the few ducks that seemed to appear from nowhere when you emerged from the trail. We'd sit on the edge of that pond laughing at the ducks and watching the ripples they made as they swam away. I'm staring at those same ripples now, but I can't smell the lilies. Only the smoke from the fire. I can't believe it's come to this. I just couldn't take it anymore. Sitting here, I struggle to remember those times with my mom...

I don't remember a lot of what we talked about on the edge of this pond but there was one very consistent refrain. She would say things like, "Imari, son. There's nothing that you will ever do, nothing that you will ever tell me, that will make me stop loving you."

"Yes, Mom. I know. I know," I'd say, rolling my eyes but smiling inside. That assurance, that constant assurance as a young boy, made me feel so tethered—a warm yellow, blinding glow of acceptance and love.

I'm sure though she wouldn't be able to forgive me for this.

_2_

IMARI

My father was a larger-than-life character born somewhere in New York—I could never remember where. It was so hard to focus on anything else when he was around. Even my own thoughts, which at five or six years old should have been solely focused on myself, were about him and how suffocating it felt to be around him. He'd always complain about how backwards this small town in Georgia was and how small-minded all the people were here.

"You know all these men here are too afraid to challenge these white boys. Always lowering their eyes to the ground when they talk to them—trying to make themselves so small so that those good ol' boys don't feel threatened. It's a damn shame."

I knew better than to say anything when he was

on one of these rants, but I would study my mother. Even though I didn't really have the vocabulary at that age to articulate this, I understood what I was seeing on my mother's face. It was shame and regret. My father had moved here with my mom to my mom's hometown. They had gone to college together in Atlanta—my father in his last year of school, my mother in her first when she got pregnant with me. Of course, I didn't find this out until I was older. What my father didn't seem to understand was that when he so vocally criticized the people of this town, he was criticizing my mother's uncles and brothers and father and, by extension, her. She knew that he blamed her for his station in life. He wanted to be a doctor or a lawyer but when they found out my mom was pregnant, my mom dropped out of school and moved in with my grandparents. He followed soon after, completing his last semester of college. He had to immediately go to work in a factory to earn money to support me and Mom, doing the exact type of work he'd gone to college to avoid—backbreaking manual labor for minimum wage. He'd leave for work very early in the morning, long before I would wake up for school, and was there long after I got home.

In the summers, when I was out of school, Mom and I would get to spend the entire day together. The best days were when she'd surprise me with an adventure. We'd quickly eat breakfast. She would have a packed lunch or a bag filled with snacks and we'd go to the zoo or on a hike or to the park. And though I had friends at school and some friends in my neighborhood, there was no one I wanted to spend time with more than my mom.

She had this well of knowledge about everything, it seemed. She'd point out different plants on our hikes or tell me how to use the sun if I got lost in the woods. I would hang on to her every word with absolute trust. Where my father's language seemed to always be so negative and always about himself, my mom's opened me up to new worlds and imparted essential skills she felt I needed to know to really understand how the world worked. We'd go on these adventures in the back of an old white Ford pickup that my dad would use to haul wood or furniture or steel. But when we used the old rusty truck, it became a chariot, leading us on adventures with outcomes unknown. Sometimes, my mom would let me sit in the back of the truck with the window behind her head cracked open and would ask me, "Where to, Prince Imari?"

It was always so sad for me when the summers came to an end and not only because it meant going back to school. It also meant the end of these wonderful summers with my mom. During the school year, I was limited to small moments with her: breakfast before school, the short car ride to school, and the few hours after school before my father got home from work. When my dad was there, my mother's focus completely shifted to taking care of him. He couldn't seem to do anything for himself. Mom did all the cooking and cleaning and was constantly running errands for him. And though I would try to follow her around on these errands, my father would always tell me to stop.

"Boy. Stop following your mother around and go outside and play. You ain't never gonna make any friends that way."

I'd look at my mom, pleading with her to save me. She would always just caress the side of my face with her hand as if to say, "I'm sorry, baby. I want you to stay too but do what your father says."

IMANI

It wasn't always this way. George was very sweet once. We'd met at a social that was being thrown by one of the fraternities over at Morehouse where George was a senior. I was a freshman at Spelman. It's funny the random things you remember about significant moments in your life. For me, I remember his cologne. I don't remember the brand, but I would certainly recognize it if I smelled it today. He had clearly put on too much of it. So much that when he finally came up to speak to me at the social after eyeing me up and down from across the room all night, I had to take a step back from him. He didn't notice though. It's so easy to look back and ascribe meaning to the smallest things. For instance, years after that moment, I thought surely that was a sign. If I had just paid attention then.... He was so oblivious to the offensive amount of cologne he had on. He didn't notice my reaction to it. This was clearly the early signs of a self-centered man. If I chose to marry him, I would spend a lifetime bending to his will.

But I was blinded and not just by the fumes from his cologne. The way he spoke about his future, filled with such hope and aspiration, it made me want to dream bigger. I was midway through my first year and had been on a few dates. They were all fine men—well, boys really. And that was it in the end. I couldn't have articulated it then but what I was witnessing in those first few moments with George were the dreams of a man. And I found it intoxicating.

Our courtship was short and I'm afraid to say that I didn't make him work very hard at it. There was a bench somewhat secluded from spying eyes where we would meet each evening. I remember how, despite the cold, I never really seemed to notice. My body was buzzing with excitement and anticipation. We held hands on that first meeting—the next he'd kissed my cheek. By the end of the first week, we were making out regularly. God, if my mother had known, she would have called me a "fast girl" and would remind me what our Lord and Savior Jesus Christ had to say about sex outside of marriage. But I had pushed my mother's words far outside my mind when I was with George. I had never really felt anything like desire before. Sure, I had posters of the Jackson Five up in my room. Jermaine was my favorite. But I had never wanted Jermaine to do to me what I wanted George to do. And I couldn't stop these thoughts. More to the point, I didn't want to.

So, it should not be a surprise that when the opportunity came for us to "go all the way," I didn't hesitate. I yearned for him to be inside of me and nothing short of that would have sufficed. In those days, finding a place to do it was as much a part of the activity as the activity itself. And there was no lingering or spooning afterwards. The stakes were too high should we have been caught. We'd found an empty supply closet on his campus. The whole deed was done in five minutes. Because I came from a very religious household, there was never any discussion about contraceptives or safe sex. It was only no sex and "do you want to burn in hell for all eternity or be welcomed by God with outstretched arms on that day?" So, of course I didn't know to ask George to wear a condom and he certainly wasn't going to suggest it. For me, it was my first time. I could tell the same wasn't true for George—the skillfulness by which he maneuvered my body—his hand deftly removing my panties and releasing my breasts from their cotton prison.

I wasn't worried though. Who gets pregnant the first time they have sex? Well, I did. I know it was from that first time because it was the only time we had sex. A couple weeks later when I was supposed to have my period, I didn't, and I was never late. We were still seeing each other but school had gotten very busy for George and, as I mentioned, he was very ambitious. I was far too embarrassed to speak a word to anyone—especially to my nosy roommate Roma who had warned me not to get involved with a senior. "Girl, all they want from you is what's between your legs—not between your ears," she had said when I'd come home from that first encounter at the fraternity social. I certainly didn't want her to say, "I told you so." And, of course, there was no way I could tell my mom. She'd force me to keep the baby whether I wanted to or not and I wasn't sure what I wanted to do. I couldn't believe something I had done for five minutes was going to change the rest of my life.

And what about George? I knew that he cared about me, despite what Roma had said. He had so many plans for his life though and I was sure being saddled with a wife and child wasn't among them.

I was frozen to the point of inaction, and I just tried to ignore it. I was always a slim girl—skinny some might say—so it was very noticeable when I started to gain weight. George liked it and when time and opportunity would arise, we were having sex.

He was insatiable in the way that all men are at that age, I guess. There was no point in resisting it now. I couldn't get more pregnant.

When the truth finally came out, it was completely unplanned—much like the pregnancy itself. On some weekends, we'd go out to a diner nearby just off campus. It was on one of these nights that what I had been ignoring and hiding in the shadows came crashing forward into the light. It was my cravings that gave me away in the end. I had never really cared for red meat and George knew this about me. I suppose he would have never noticed this if he himself wasn't such a lover of red meat. He'd even remarked on this when we started dating, how crazy he thought it was that I didn't like steak and burgers. There was just something about seeing people saw away at a bloody steak that had always turned my stomach.

But there was something about red meat that I just couldn't get enough of at this stage in my pregnancy so when I ordered it at the diner that night, George noticed.

"What? You're eating a steak?"

It hadn't even occurred to me that I should keep my newly attained appetite for red meat a secret. I searched my mind for a plausible excuse. The best I came up with in the moment was, "I guess you're rubbing off on me."

But George wouldn't let it go.

"Nah. You hated steak. I've never seen you eat a bite of red meat and now, all of a sudden, you're ordering a steak? A burger maybe, but steak?"

"What can I tell you?" I was dying to change the subject. "Are you ready for midterms?"

"Why are you trying to change the subject?"

"I'm not," I said, trying to sound light. "It's just not that big a deal."

"But it is a big deal," he said, searching his brain when he finally landed on something. "You know, the only other time I've seen something like this was when my sister was pregnant. She started eating—"

His voice caught.

"No. No. No. You aren't. Please. Shit. No. No."

"No what? What are you talking about?" I said but I couldn't even make eye contact with him at this point.

"I can't believe this. Oh god. Oh god. What are you going to do? You can't keep it."

I'm not sure why I was immediately defensive. I hadn't even decided if I wanted to keep it at that point, though I was getting closer to the point where my indecision was going to be a decision.

"I can't?"

"You'll ruin your life. Hell, you'll ruin my life."

And there it was really. He wasn't really concerned about me, was he? This was about him.

"It's not really up to you, though, is it?"

"Please, Imani. You have to be reasonable here.

You can't take care of a baby by yourself. You haven't even finished your first year of school. I know you can't tell those religious parents of yours. They'll disown you."

I knew he was right about all of this but, in that moment, it just felt like an attack.

"How quickly this has turned into my failing and my responsibility. Should I assume that to mean you don't intend on taking any responsibility now or in the future?"

"Jesus, Imani."

"There's no point bringing him into this."

"Oh, for fuck's sake!"

People around us started to look up from their meals, noticing our argument.

"Keep your voice down," I said, worrying that someone around us might hear that I was pregnant and that the news would travel sixty miles northwest to my mother and father.

"I'm not throwing away my life for you."

"I see. I have your decision then," I said, gathering my things as the waitress returned to the table. "I'll take my meal to go please, miss."

"Of course," she said with a knowing look that said that she'd seen this all before. I suppose in her line of work, she was constantly on the fringe of huddled conversations and lives being changed forever. Just another day for her.

In the end, I had to tell my parents who, in turn, contacted George's parents in New York. While not as religious as my parents, George's parents had a strong sense of doing what was right. My parents had only wanted George to be financially responsible for our child but didn't want him anywhere near me. In fact, they had forbidden it. He had already ruined my life enough, thank you very much. He would not ruin the life of their grandchild. They said George should finish college and go on to grad school and medical school. But as soon as he was finished, he would need to take care of his responsibilities. George's parents thought this was fair and encouraged their son to continue his education. But it infuriated him to have our parents making decisions about his life. And he knew why my parents wanted him to go to medical school—so our child could get more money. Well, he was having none of that. Instead, he would finish his undergrad but that was it. He wasn't going to follow their plan. He moved to my small town and asked me to marry him.

"Ok, little girl. You have a decision to make. You wanna marry that man, go right ahead. But you will no longer be a part of this family," my mother had said.

"Ugenia, honey. Aren't you being a little too rough on the girl?" my father had said.

But I knew who made the decisions in that house. She had drawn a line in the sand.

"I mean it. You will be forbidden from contacting your siblings and certainly not us. You want that life with that awful man, go and have it. But don't come crawling back to us when you realize what a horrible mistake you've made."

"Hmm. Is that what Jesus would do?" I said, which earned me a slap across my face—drawing blood. And that was it. That was the last time I spoke to my mother for many years.

3

IMARI

When my father was on a rant like this, I would just sneak across the street to our path and go to see the ducks. They seemed to always know when it was just me—hanging back on the opposite side of the pond. After all, I had no food for them. I would just sit there trying to remember the stories my mom had told me, some real, some imagined, as I skipped rocks around the pond. If the ducks had a little sympathy and came to say hello, I would talk to them. I'd pretend they were my siblings, and we were all here together. They'd prompt me to get into the water, but I'd tell them that Mom didn't want us swimming in the pond without her—that they were going to get us into trouble.

It was during one of these conversations when I

was around nine years old that I heard some rustling in the trees behind me. Jumping up and startling my duck siblings, I yelled out, "Mom, is that you?" The person who emerged from the path was not my mom but instead a little blonde-haired girl— her hair in a ponytail swinging back and forth as she approached me.

"Who were you talking to?" she asked.

Embarrassed that I had been caught, I simply said, "No one. How did you find the path?"

"Oh, well, I saw you when you came in. I did get turned around some when I got into the woods. It's so cool in there. Do you come here a lot?" I didn't really want to answer this girl. I felt like I was betraying my mom. This was our place. Now that this girl knew about it, who would she tell?

She seemed to sense my hesitation. "I won't tell anyone about this place if that's what's you're worried about."

"Ok," I said.

"My name is Andrea. My dad's name is Andrew. I think he wanted a son but he got me instead. So, I guess I'm something like a junior. What's your name?"

"Imari." I wasn't going to tell her that I was also named after one of my parents. My mom's name is Imani and since my dad didn't move down here to Georgia until after I was born, my mother got to name me. I was hoping this girl would take the hint from my short answers that I wanted to be left alone but she persisted.

"Wow. What a cool name! Black kids always have the coolest names. My best friend at school is named LeTangia. Isn't that a cool name?" I didn't really feel like I needed to answer her question as she quickly continued. "I mean, I like my name and that I'm named after my dad but it's not a cool name. What do you do here? Do you ever get into the water? Is it safe? Oh! There are ducks!" she said, noticing them for the first time. "Do you feed them?"

She had asked so many questions, I didn't know where to start.

"I talk a lot, huh? My dad says I'll make a good lawyer but I don't want to do that. They are all men anyway. I've never seen any women lawyers on TV commercials. Have you? I think I want to do something more exciting than that. I want to travel the world. I was watching a show, National Geographic or something. Did you know there are women in Africa who carry large baskets on their heads? It's crazy. They don't use their hands either. Anyway, I'd love to see that in person. And I want to see a penguin and not in a zoo but where they actually live."

It seemed the only way I was going to get out of this interaction was to leave.

"Well, I have to get home."

"Oh ok," she said, looking a little sad.

"It was nice to meet you," I said—hoping this

would make up for my rudeness.

Her face brightened and she said, "Can I walk with you? I got a little lost before..."

"Sure."

I led her through the path, understanding that by doing so I was all but assuring that I would see her here again. Nothing to be done about that now.

"We just moved into the house up the street from you. My dad sells insurance and got relocated here from Florida. Dad says Florida was such a goldmine—you know, with all the old people. But he feels like we can have a good life here too. What does your dad do?"

"He works in a factory building something. I don't really know."

"Oh, that's cool. How is he? As a dad, I mean. Is he mean or strict? My dad is a pushover. I just sit in his lap and say, 'Please, please, Daddy,' and he melts. I don't think he's ever raised his voice to me."

"My dad definitely isn't a pushover."

As we stepped out of the woods from behind the dogwood tree, I quickly started up the driveway to my house, yelling over my shoulder, "Was nice meeting you. Gotta run!"

"Nice meeting you too. Maybe I'll see you at school tomorrow. I think we probably go to the same school. Are you in the fourth grade?"

"Yep. See you tomorrow."

As I entered the house, I was immediately met by

my dad, who looked at me disapprovingly. "Boy, I know I told you to make friends but you better be careful with that one."

He must have seen me walking up the driveway talking to Andrea. "She's not my friend."

"Well, probably best to keep it that way. White women ain't nothin' but trouble."

I was tired of this conversation. So, I turned and walked past my mom who was in the kitchen listening in on our conversation as she prepared for dinner. I could tell she wanted to ask me questions, but she also didn't want to encourage any more commentary from my father.

IMANI

I had so much hope for our future when we first started out in that humble, shotgun-styled house on the south side of town. The yard, well, there wasn't much of one really. It was more dirt than anything else. George's parents had loaned us the money for the down payment. While they were disappointed, they were good people and wanted us to be happy. They had George late in life, so they were already in their sixties and not in particularly good health. But they would send money when they could and would call every Sunday at 4:00 p.m. without fail.

At first, George looked for office jobs in law offices and at hospitals. They were always interested in him on the phone but after a little scrutiny of his resume, they would discover where he went to school and know that he was a black man. In those days here in the south, there were certain types of jobs a black man could have where he could actually support his family and working in the local electric factory was the main one. But George resisted this truth. He continued to go after these jobs meant for white people and would get turned down over and over. And I wanted to support his endeavor to find an office job. I did. But we had bills and needed formula and diapers and our money from his parents was not going to sustain us.

"Honey, I know you don't want to hear this, but I think you may just need to take a factory job. Just for a while. You can still apply to—"

"But that's just it. If I give in now, I'll be stuck in that place for the rest of my life. I know it. No one is going to let me take off work to go on an interview for another job."

I hated to admit it, but he was probably right. But I needed to convince him to do it anyway.

"You know, there must be management roles there at the electric factory."

"Sure. But who do you think those jobs are going to?"

In the end, he caved and started working at the electric factory building electronic components of some kind. It was hard work and it seemed to chip away at his soul each day. I spent my days with my little man, Imari. He had his father's eyes.

I guess that's what all new parents do in the beginning—try to see who their child most looks like. Imari had gotten the best of both of us. He had my high cheek bones and darker chocolate complexion while he had his father's strong chin and beautiful soft brown eyes. It was always so conflicting to look into the same pair of eyes and yet have them provoke two different emotions. When I stared in Imari's eyes, they were filled with curiosity and love but when I stared at George's, I saw resentment and an ever-dimming light.

Soon, we fell into a routine and there was certainly some comfort in that, but I was worried all the time. George had been such an ambitious man. He could talk on various topics with such eloquence but increasingly his language started to change and his tone as well. I suppose, though he never told me this, that the other men at the factory would have teased him about his college education. "You spent all that time, effort, and money in college and are in the same spot as me, brotha." Of course, he would have had to abandon his properly worded sentences for fear of being labeled an "Uncle Tom" or "talking white." And naturally the conversations at the factory would be representative of the plight all of them shared—their common experience of wanting more out of their lives but continuing to have those dreams demolished at the hands of white men.

George would come home and just continue this conversation with me—about how unfair things were and how disappointing it was to see his brothers just lay down and accept their fate.

"You should see these men. Strong, black men, lowering their eyes and saying, 'Yes sir, no sir,' all the damn time—like tortured puppies in a cage. I fucking can't stand it."

"George, I know things aren't the same here as they were for you in New York. You know, I don't have anything keeping me here anymore—now that my family has disowned me. Why don't we move to New York and live near your parents?"

At this, I saw a shimmer of light in his eyes. "Really? You would move to New York?"

"Yes. Of course. I never really wanted to move back here. I just didn't feel like I had a choice. But now..."

"Wow. You don't know how happy this makes me, Imari."

"It's so good to see you happy. I don't think I've seen you smile in such a long time."

As I said this, George pulled me toward him— his hands made course from the factory. He slid the skinny straps of my sundress off my shoulders and let it fall to the ground. He was all over me like he'd spawned an extra pair of hands. I was back in the supply closet at Morehouse. I could smell the floor cleaner—the musty smell of the mop—when suddenly I heard, "Mommy?"

But George wasn't going to stop.

"I should—"

"Leave him."

"But—"

"Please. Imani." His passion erupted and we were back to the present. He gave me a gentle kiss to seal the moment. "We're going to be so happy."

4

IMARI

Monday morning while eating breakfast, Mom found her opportunity to chat me up.

"So, tell me about your new friend. What's her name?"

"Andrea. Her father's name is Andrew and they just moved into the brickhouse at the top of the street."

"Oh, right! The Jeffersons' old house. And Andrea. Such a pretty name. Is she nice?"

"She's fine. Talks a lot." Reluctantly, I continued, "And...she found our trail and the pond." I looked at my mom now to see if I noticed any betrayal in her face.

Instead, she smiled a little and seemed to measure her words. "That's ok, baby. As you get older, you're going to want to spend more time with kids your own age and less with me."

"That's not true," I interrupted. "I don't need any friends, Mom. I have you." At this, my mom got up from her chair and gave me a big hug from behind.

"Of course, baby. You'll always have me. But you don't have to feel guilty if you make new friends. It's very healthy to have many friends and friends who are your age. It'll all happen in time. No need to rush it."

"I can't wait until the summer when we have time to go on our adventures again in the old chariot."

"Speaking of the chariot, have you come up with a name for it?"

"Hmmm..." I had considered this a lot but nothing seemed to really suit it. "Maybe, 'The Voyageur'?"

"'The Voyageur'...I like it! Now. Finish your breakfast so I can run you to school."

I finished breakfast and went to brush my teeth and grab my school bag. I glanced out the window to see Andrea standing alone at the bus stop. A small part of me felt bad that she was standing there alone.

As we climbed into the truck, my mom also noticed Andrea standing at the bus stop and I already knew what was coming.

"Go and ask your friend if she wants a ride with us to school."

"Oh, Mom. Do I have to?"

"She's at that bus stop all by herself. Now I know

I taught you to be more of a gentleman than that."

My eyes found the ground at this chastisement. I never wanted to feel my mom's disapproval. It was the worst feeling in the world.

Sulking away toward the bus stop, I saw Andrea waving.

"Hi, Imari! Is that your mom? What's her last name?"

"Johnson."

"Hi, Mrs. Johnson," she yelled.

My mom, who was watching this interaction, waved back to her.

"My mom wants to know if you'd like to ride with us to school."

"Really!? That would be great!!" She hooked her arm into mine.

Begrudgingly, I walked with her back to my mom.

"Hi, Mrs. Johnson. Thanks so much for the ride to school. I'm so nervous about starting in a new school. My dad left for work already and my mom is looking after my little brother Jeffrey. He's only eight months old."

"Well, we're happy to have you, Andrea. Climb on in. We don't want to be late. Imari, get the door for her, son."

I opened the door and let Andrea climb in between me and my mom. These trips to school were some of the only alone time I got with my mom during the school year and now this girl was stealing it from me.

Andrea talked almost non-stop. From time to time, my mom would interject by trying to pull me into the conversation. "Isn't that nice, Imari?" she'd say, or some version of that. To which I would simply respond, "Yes ma'am." As we pulled up to school, I was anxious to get out of the truck and put this car ride to an end.

"Have a great day at school, you two! Imari, honey, you make sure Andrea knows where to go today. Ok?"

"Yes ma'am."

"Thanks, Mrs. Johnson!"

"You're welcome, dear. I'll be here at 3:30 to pick you both up."

Great. This was officially a thing now. We're riding to and from school together.

Andrea appeared to be reading my mind again. "I'm sorry. I didn't mean to talk so much on the ride. You probably didn't want me to come with you, huh? It's ok. I know I'm a lot to deal with. My dad says it's going to take a very patient man that's gonna want to marry me. He always laughs when he says it so I know he's kidding but it feels like the truth. Anyway, if you don't want me to ride with you, you can just say. I won't be mad."

Right. My mom would know right away and I'd be met with more disapproving looks that sliced away at my heart.

"It's ok. Come on. I'll show you to Ms. Jenkins'

class. She's our teacher."

"Oh, thanks, Imari! You're so nice."

IMANI

Reenergized, George started making calls to his parents. They were both so happy that we were going to be moving to New York. We were looking in the Queens borough to be close to them. George's mom Janice and his dad James knew an older couple who were looking to sell their place to move in with their daughter in Harlem.

"Oh baby, it would be perfect. It's so close, you could walk here. And I know she'd give you a good deal on it, seeing as how they movin' in with their daughter. I'm so excited, baby," Janice had said in one of those calls.

"Think you could send us some pictures of the house?" George asked.

"Oh, that's a good idea, baby. Well, now, you know I don't really walk that much no mo and ya dad—well, he ain't been feeling too good, baby."

"Really? What's going on? Is he ok?"

"Oh, well, he doesn't want me to worry you." In the background, you could hear James coughing as he made his way to the phone. "Here's your father."

"George, son?" he said, voice raspy, likely from coughing.

"Hey, Dad. How are you feeling?"

"Well, son. You know. I used to get colds all the time, ya know. They just harder to get over when you're older, son."

"I hear ya, Dad. Have you been to the doctor?"

"Aw. None of that now. You sound like your mother." James laughed a little and started to cough uncontrollably, so much that he couldn't continue talking and Janice had to take the phone.

"I don't know, Mom. He doesn't sound good. Are you sure he shouldn't just go to the doctor?"

"You know your dad. He's not going to go."

"Maybe you should make him."

At this, it was Janice's turn to laugh. "You're funny, boy. If I could make your father do what I wanted, the first thing to go would be that recliner of his."

They were both laughing now. George was looking over at me as I listened in to this loving family. I envied the relationship George had with his parents. It was going to mean so much to all of them to be reunited.

The next morning, George kissed me goodbye as he headed off to work. Imari was in his highchair eating his Cheerios—getting more on the floor than in his mouth. He was walking now and was going to say his first words soon, I knew it.

It was going to be a scorcher that day. Highs expected to crack the hundreds. I was about to take Imari out of his highchair to clean him up when the phone rang.

"Hello?"

"Imani, sweetheart? Has George left for work?"

"Oh yes. He left ages ago. I'm just here feeding Imari. You should see the state of him," I said, laughing.

I stopped cold when I realized that Janice was crying.

"Janice? Is everything ok?"

At this, Janice fell apart. She was trying to talk but I couldn't make out what she was saying. "Wouldn't—wouldn't—wake up—"

"Wouldn't wake up? Who wouldn't wake up, Janice?"

"James. He wouldn't wake up."

"Oh, god! Janice, you have to call 911 right now!"

"I did, sweetheart. He's gone."

I had to call George at work. I could hear the loud noises of the factory in the background. I had never been inside the factory, but I would occasionally drop George off when his car was in the shop. I had imagined the gritty scene in my head many times—piecing it together from the men I saw leaving when I would pick him up and the noises I would hear over the phone on the rare occasion I would call. The last time I called, Imari had a 102 temp, and I was terrified. With no real support network, George was the only one I could call but he wasn't happy about it.

"You can't call me here at work, Mani," a nick-name he would reserve for when he was most irritated with me.

Today would be different. All these small moments in a life, insignificant in the amount of time—minutes, sometimes seconds—yet powerful enough to tear away a piece of your soul and change the course of your life forever. And here I was, again, being the person to deliver this to him.

"Imani? Baby, you know—"

"George, you need to come home."

"Why? What's happened?"

5

IMARI

Andrea asked many questions as we walked to our class and I tried to answer them all so that when she reported back to my mom, she'd know I'd been a good boy. As we entered our classroom, Ms. Jenkins lit up.

"Oh, great! You have a friend already. Andrea Antenelli, right, honey? Do you go by Andrea?"

"Yes."

Watching, I was so shocked to see Andrea short of words, my mouth fell open. She must have been telling the truth about how nervous she was.

"Fortunately, there's an empty desk at the back of the class next to Imari. Have a seat, sweetheart, and we'll start class soon."

"Ok. Thanks."

Enjoying this newfound restraint of tongue, I went to my desk and pulled out my notebook. Andrea must have gotten a list of needed supplies sent to her parents because she followed my lead and pulled out a similar notebook with pockets in the back for storing handouts for homework.

The first half of the day went by normally. Andrea seemed to be following along ok. When Ms. Jenkins called on her to answer math questions, she had no problem producing the correct answer. She was definitely smarter than me.

It was now time for lunch, which I personally hated. All the groups of friends sat together at their tables. I mostly sat by myself but sometimes my play cousin, Monica, would sit with me when she was mad at one of her friends. She was my "play cousin" because we weren't actually related but our parents were very close and would occasionally go on small trips together. And because we were the same age, we got stuck together along with her two younger siblings, a boy and a girl, Michael and Mahalia, born fourteen months apart. Mostly, Monica seemed to tolerate me more than anything.

Unfortunately, today was one of those days and I had Andrea following me around everywhere too. This brought me unwanted attention from the other boys in the class.

"Oh, look! Imari has two new girlfriends!"

"Shut up, Bruce! That's my cousin!" Monica said.

"He ain't yo real cousin."

"So! At least I don't still wet the bed. You baby! Got your diaper on today, baby?"

I stole a quick glance at Andrea who had her head down as if trying to pretend none of this was happening. Bruce quickly moved away at this insult. There's probably nothing worse at the age of nine than to be accused of still wetting the bed. Even worse for Bruce, he was eleven years old, having been held back a few times already. And there had been many eyewitnesses to his weak bladder during a school lock-in back in the Fall.

Andrea seemed relieved that this was over and felt comfortable enough again to start talking. "Is everyone here so mean?"

"I don't know," I said. "I guess that was pretty normal for me. I mostly just stay out of it and people mostly leave me alone—which is how I like it."

"Don't you get lonely?"

I considered this for a moment. "I'd rather be lonely than laughed at."

"Hmmm. I think maybe you just haven't had a real friend. Good friends, the real ones—they're the best. I miss my best friend LeTangia. My parents gave me money for stamps so I can write to her. I wish I could call her though, but my parents say no. That her parents can't afford the long distance—whatever that means."

"There's a cost to make calls to people in other states and countries."

"Really? How do you know that?"

"TV commercials." I smiled.

IMANI

George was home and was frantic trying to pack a bag for the Greyhound he'd have to catch in Atlanta. I wanted to come with him, but he said it would just be too much for me with a small child on a bus for nearly twenty-four hours. He gave me a gentle kiss on his way out the door.

"I'll call in a couple of days," he said.

"Ok, sweetheart. We both love you. Let me know if you need anything."

I could see the overwhelming sadness and regret in his eyes—likely thinking that he should have been there, that he could have convinced his father to go to the hospital. He was also concerned about his job. While he hated it, it was a good-paying job and the only one of that kind that he could find. As such, there were men, many of them, waiting in the wings to take that job from him. His boss had said as much to him when he called asking to take the week off.

"This is the last time, Johnson. Sorry for your loss and all but we got a business to run here."

For me, I was of course upset for George that he had lost his father, but I felt like something else was lost too. Just days ago, we were both excited for our future. How would George be after this? It made me think of my own father. I know he was just following my mother's orders not to speak to me. It was a small town though and occasionally I'd see them in town. My father would look at me, hopeful and longing to see me and his grandson, but my mother would just pull him away.

Life is so short and what's done is done. It seems cruel now, on the part of my mother, to continue to lay this burden on all of us. We're going to blink, and this life will be over and what would have been the point of all this?

But when I was feeling down about my situation, I would just look at my beautiful boy—full of wonder and excitement—and it would soothe the torn threads of my heart. He was so blissfully unaware of the world he was being born into and I hoped to keep it that way for him for as long as I possibly could. I couldn't imagine my life without this one. He was becoming a fixture on my hip or at my elbow and I didn't want it any other way.

Yesterday, while out exploring the woods looking for blackberry bushes for a pie I was going to bake, I saw what must have been an old game trail—the ground well-worn and the brush pushed away. Curiosity got the better of me and I continued to follow the trail to the end and boy, what a good decision that was. First, there were blackberry bushes abound in the clearing. And second, there was a lovely little pond surrounded by lovely flowers—lilies, I think. I took one to ask Mrs. Jefferson at the top of the street. She loved all things gardening and would know right away. For all my creativity and book smarts, the skill of gardening and growing things alluded me.

Imari and I sat on the edge of that pond eating blackberries that I cut into small pieces for him with the knife I'd brought with me. The place felt so magical—like it had been sitting here eagerly waiting to be found. And without thinking about it, I started telling Imari a story—one that would fit the majesty of our surroundings. He was still too young to quite understand me, but it seemed like he was hanging on to my every word.

It was time to get Imari back home for his nap, so I made my way back through the trail and made a note to myself of where the trail started. I intended to make this a regular thing—our trips to the pond. As I was walking up the driveway, I could hear the phone ringing. I took off for the door with Imari in tow, trying to make it to the phone before it stopped ringing. I knew it was George because no one else ever called.

"Hello? George?" I said, panting between each word.

"Where have you been? I've been calling for an hour?"

"Sorry, sweetheart. We were just out—"

"She's gone."

"What? Who's gone?"

"My mother." At this, he broke down.

I was trying to understand but it was difficult. I knew that it was bad. She hadn't just gone missing. She was dead. I insisted that he let me come to him, but he wouldn't hear of it. There was too much to do now with both his parents gone. He had no time to grieve. He would have to put it aside and get done what needed to be done. He had extended family there too and they would help as much as they could—to clean out his parents' home to make arrangements for the memorial service that would need to happen on Saturday so that George could spend Sunday traveling back home.

I felt like a horrible wife—not being there for my husband while he said goodbye to his parents. Maybe I should have just gone anyway—but George was very clear that he didn't want me there. He didn't have the capacity to worry about one more thing. Maybe I could have helped relieve some of the things on his plate.

When I had a chance to really step away and think about it, I began to understand why he didn't want me there. He'd said as much to me on the phone. He didn't have time to grieve. He felt comfortable being emotional around me. If I was there, he'd be compelled to allow his grief in and he'd be trapped in that grief, without the ability to get done all the things he needed to. In a way, I felt like it was such a privilege that he felt so safe to be vulnerable around me. On the other hand, I still felt like I was not doing part of my primary responsibilities—like I was letting him down.

It wasn't until George returned late Sunday night that I heard the details of what had happened to his mother. George had arrived at their family home on Tuesday evening. He had knocked on the door for a while but then let himself in with a key that he still had. He'd assumed his mother was sleeping. He'd come in and put his stuff in his childhood bedroom that still had some of the wooden toys of his youth scattered about. He'd made his way to his mother's bedroom. He'd tried to wake her to let her know he had arrived, but she wouldn't wake. Panicked, he'd phoned 911. She was pronounced dead on arrival. It wasn't until the coroner had left and the funeral home had come to reunite his mother and father that he'd discovered the note on the kitchen counter.

My Dearest George,

I know this will be very hard on you, but I cannot go on living without your father. Maybe if I had made him go to the hospital, we would all have been here reunited again—you, your wife, and your beautiful son, Imari. I will hate to not see him grow up. Be good to your wife, baby. I hope you can know a love like the one me and your father have. Now, I must go and be with him. I can't have him wandering around heaven on his own. You know he's useless without me.

I love you, son.
Mom

6

IMARI

The rest of the day proceeded without incident, and it was time to go home. Ms. Jenkins stopped us as we were leaving.

"Andrea. Do you know which bus to get on?"

"Yes. But I'm riding home with Imari."

"Oh, great. Well, great job today, honey. We'll see you tomorrow."

"Thanks, Ms. Jenkins. See you tomorrow!"

My mom was parked on the curb at the front of the school. When she saw us, she got out of the truck and went to wave when I saw her stumble a little. I ran to her and then slowed as I approached.

"Hi, Mom. Are you ok?"

"Oh, yes, baby. I'm fine. I jumped up a little too

fast is all. How was your first day, Andrea?"

I had forgotten she was there.

"Just fine, Mrs. Johnson. Ms. Jenkins is so sweet."

"And were all the kids nice to you?"

Andrea and I quickly stole glances at each other. I hoped she was still reading my mind. The last thing I wanted her to do was to be honest about the kids in school. As far as my mom knew, I was well liked with a few friends, and everyone was very nice.

"They were ok. I definitely miss my best friend back in Florida, LeTangia. Imari was very nice to me though and let me sit with him at lunch and introduced me to Monica."

Now, none of that was true. Monica didn't speak to either of us really—more at us. And it wasn't like I asked her to join me for lunch. She just sat down. But I certainly wasn't going to correct her. She was earning me brownie points with my mom.

"That was very sweet, Imari. See? I knew I'd raised you to be a gentleman."

As we pulled up to Andrea's house and I jumped out of the car to let her out, my mom got out of the car too.

"Andrea, are your parents home?"

"My mom is home looking after my little brother."

"Well, I'd like to meet her please. Would you let her know I'm here?"

"Ok."

Andrea disappeared inside.

Moments later, Andrea's mom appeared, looking a little disheveled with a baby on her hip—presumably Andrea's little brother.

"Hello. Andrea tells me you wanted to meet me?"

"Yes. Hello," my mother said as she approached with her hand outstretched. "I'm Imani and this here is my son Imari. Imari, son, come here."

I approached shyly. "Hi, Mrs. Antenelli," I said as I tucked in behind my mother.

"Hi. I'm Mary."

"I gave Andrea a ride to school and back home today, so I just wanted to make sure you knew that and were fine with that—and to introduce myself and Imari to you."

"Well, that's certainly nice of you but it's not necessary. Andrea is perfectly fine riding the bus."

Hearing this, Andrea pleaded with her mom. "Mom, please. Imari is my only friend at the school. There's no one else at the bus stop with me in the morning and I'd be riding the bus with a bunch of kids I don't know!"

"Andrea. Don't argue with me."

"Mom, please. Dad would let me."

My mom interjected. "I really don't mind. And Imari likes the company too."

At this all eyes were on me. This was my chance to get my mom back to myself but I made the mistake of looking at Andrea who seemed to be on the verge of tears.

"Andrea has been great company, Mrs. Antenelli."

Little Jeffrey, who had been looking around at all the new faces initially, was now impatiently wiggling in his mother's arms. This seemed to settle things for Mrs. Antenelli.

"Well, fine. But you'll have to make sure your dad is ok with it."

Lighting up, she said, "Thanks, Mom!"

The next morning, as I was sitting at the small round table in the kitchen eating my cereal and talking to Mom, I heard a small knock at the front door.

"Imari, grab that will you? It's probably Andrea."

Getting up from the table and leaving my cereal—which was already dangerously close to getting soggy—I went to the front door and opened it. As my mom suspected, Andrea was standing there looking a little coy and anxious to come in.

"Hi, Imari, can I come in?" Andrea said but didn't really wait for a response.

"I'm guessing your dad said ok."

"Yep. He's totally fine with it."

I led Andrea through the dining room into the kitchen where my mom was busy making my lunch.

"Good morning, Andrea, dear. Have you had breakfast?"

"Yes ma'am," Andrea said as she eyed my Lucky Charms. "Oh, I love Lucky Charms! My mom won't let me eat them. Says there too much sugar. It's just

Raisin Bran for me. Though I put a load of sugar on them when she isn't looking." Andrea seemed amused by her own admission.

"Well, have a seat. We'll be ready to leave shortly."

And that was it. The beginning of a new routine of Andrea showing up just as I was finishing breakfast. She would talk incessantly about nothing and hog all the free time with my mom. Then, she'd come home with us and hang around after we arrived home for a while. My mom insisted that we both start on our homework right away so that we could have as much time as possible to play. That was fine by me because by the time we had finished homework, Andrea would jump up and head home. It was also helpful having her around when I was working on word problems in Math. While I was reluctant to ask for her help initially, I got over that quickly when I realized that if I just got her help, I could be done with homework sooner and I could have a little bit of time with my mom before my dad got home from work. We went on like this for weeks and, after a while, I didn't mind it at all.

IMANI

The window had seemingly closed on our chance for happiness. I did try to connect with George—to let him know that he still had so much to live for, so much in his life to be grateful for—but it was all met with silence. I wasn't going to give up on him though. I couldn't. I was not going to let my spiteful mother be proven right. And, perhaps more importantly, I loved George and I knew, if he would just open his heart to us, that we could make him happy. Even Imari tried but the little man learned quickly that his efforts to connect with his father were fruitless.

I couldn't devote all my time to George. I had this beautiful, smart, inquisitive boy to raise and I needed him to know what unconditional love felt like. I never wanted him to feel the pain of what it felt like to be rejected by his own mother, such an unnatural feeling. You know that her blood runs in you. In a way, when a mother rejects her child, it's like the mother is rejecting a part of herself. No. Imari would never have to endure that. Perhaps I would be overcompensating in the process but is there really such thing as too much love?

Imari would be starting Kindergarten and he was so excited about it.

"Mommy, will there be other kids there like me?"

"Oh baby, there is no one in this world like you."

Imari laughed. "Mommy! I mean like the same years old. With mommies and daddies?"

"Well, there are all sorts of families, Imari. Some have mommies and daddies with no children. Some have just a mommy and children and no daddy—"

"Like us sometimes."

"Like us? But you have a father, Imari."

He seemed to be thinking this over in his six-year-old brain. "Hmmm. Only when I do something bad. Like spill milk or laugh too loud."

"Baby, I know you won't understand this now, but your father has been through a lot. He wasn't always this way. I wish you could have known him then, when he was filled with hope and was so sweet to me."

"Daddy was sweet?"

"Yes. Yes, he was."

I was starting to see now that Imari would likely never know that version of his father. It had been years now since his parents passed and I didn't recognize this man in my house. I do still try to let him know what it feels like to have a supportive wife and there are small moments. Moments where I think, there he is! But then, it's gone again. And he seems intent on crushing any hope out of his son. I know he's not making this decision consciously, but it's clear to me what he's doing and why. George had an understanding now of what his life would be like, and he had received the message—there is no hope for the Black man in America. There is no point in having dreams or loving your family. It will all just be ripped away from you. Better to just not have any dreams or love at all.

7

IMARI

I'm not sure how or when it happened exactly but this annoyingly talkative girl was now my friend in earnest. I started to enjoy the way she could fill the room with her energy and seemed to always be so upbeat and positive. And after a time, I started to ask her to stick around after we had finished our homework.

"I should go home and change out of my school clothes. My mom gets worried if I don't check in right after school."

"Ok," I said, surprisingly let down by her response. "Well, it's starting to stay light longer now, so come back by if you want."

"Ok! Gotta run," she said as she made her way to the front door.

I stood there and watched her leave just as the bus drove by. An idea started to form in my head, but I wasn't sure. I was going to need to get more evidence.

The next day when we got home from school, I checked the time on my Casio watch. It was 4:25 p.m. We only lived ten minutes from school and usually got home around 3:40 p.m. At 4:30 p.m., Andrea checked her watch and started to head for the door.

"I'll see you tomorrow, Imari. Gotta get home."

I walked Andrea to the front door and watched her walk away just as the bus drove past.

The next day while at lunch and sitting alone together, I summoned the courage to ask Andrea the question I'd been sitting on for a day.

"Hey. I notice you always leave my house at 4:30 p.m. on the dot. Did your dad really say it was ok to ride with me to school?"

I watched Andrea to see if she was going to be offended by this question or come up with a lie when she looked up and said, "No. I never asked him."

"You never asked him?"

"My mom is so busy with my brother and my dad is so busy with his new job, they don't really care about what I do—as long as I stay out of trouble. I didn't want to take the chance of my dad saying no and having to ride the bus instead. My mom probably already knows now that our moms are hanging out all the time. It's just that I started with the lie and now I just feel the need to keep it going. I just thought because you're a boy that my mom wouldn't let me hang out with you at first. But now, all she talks about is what a good influence you are on me. Like I needed a good influence or something. Really?" Andrea rolled her eyes. "Are you going to tell your mom?"

I had to consider this. While I hated the idea of lying to my mom, I had really come to enjoy our new routine and spending time with my new friend.

"No. I won't tell."

That moment seemed to cement our friendship. It seemed, at least when I was a kid, you weren't ever truly friends until you shared a secret—one big enough to get both of you into trouble.

IMANI

Imari was my world now, but I was very careful not to let George feel that. When George was around, I made it all about him. Even though Imari was young, I had the sense that he could understand that this is what I had to do as a wife. George needed to feel like the most important thing in this house because he certainly didn't feel that way when he left. And there were only small windows where we were all together with George working so early and getting off so late. If Imari didn't understand, I hoped he would when he was older.

I was a little concerned, though, about Imari. Had I given him too much of my love and affection? He didn't really seem too interested in making friends as a kid. Of course, I could understand. Kids can be vicious. I'd heard them one day when I was picking him up from school making fun of him—calling him a momma's boy. Initially I thought, *Well, what's wrong with that? He is my boy.* But I understood what they really meant. That he was weak. I knew that wasn't true. What they had categorized as weakness was really empathy, insightfulness, and love.

I did need to encourage him to make friends and that he shouldn't see it as a betrayal of any sort to find some. I couldn't have imagined though, when that friend did show up, that she'd be wrapped in white skin and blonde hair. I knew his father would take issue with this. But I'd heard them talking while at the foot of our driveway that first time they met. She was smart and extroverted. This would be good for him, and I was going to encourage it. I was a little worried about her parents. What would they think about their precious girl running around with a little black boy? Wars have been started for less. I was going to make sure I met her parents as soon as possible.

After Imari was in school, I'd go about my day—cleaning the house and doing whatever shopping needed to be done. I'd run into other moms out there doing the same and we'd stop and chat. But I hadn't really made space in my own life to nurture any of those relationships. When did I have the time? George would never allow me to go out in the evening, leaving him with Imari. It was very clear that Imari was my responsibility. I did find time though, on occasion, to go and get my hair and nails done. It was always an issue with George. He'd say stuff like, "It must be nice to be able to lay around all day and get your nails done. How much of my money did you spend on that?"

I needed to have those moments and I would pay the price of a few negative comments from George. There seemed to be more and more of those types of comments recently.

"You're getting a little thick. Maybe you should join one of those mommy walking clubs?"

I wanted to say, "You're not really a picture of physical fitness either!" But he did have a point. I was starting to gain a little weight, which was weird. I was certainly active enough with all I did running the household and I ate healthier than anyone in the house. The past few weeks, though, I had noticed that my jeans were getting a little tighter. I couldn't be pregnant. When I gave birth to Imari, the doctor had said I had issues with my ovaries, endometriosis, and it was unlikely that I would ever conceive again. Because of that, we didn't bother with birth control and for these past nine years, there hadn't even been a close call. My period hit in the second week of the month like clockwork. And while we had insurance, there was no way I could just go to the doctor without getting George involved. He held the insurance card and would never let me make a copy or even write down the group and policy information. I could, however, take a home pregnancy test and I would, just to be sure.

It was summer now and George was at work all day leaving me alone a lot with Imari. He had a new friend now, Andrea. What a pair these two made. I could tell that Imari was resisting this friendship and was even feeling guilty for not spending as much time with me as he used to—but this is the way. We give birth—hold them in our body for months, in our arms for years and then, must let them go. I loved that this process was slower than most of the other moms I would talk to—especially with their sons. By age six or seven, their sons were already pulling away, they would tell me. I'd hear this and feel conflicted. I loved that I wasn't going through this myself, but I was also worried that we were becoming a bit codependent. For all intents and purposes, Imari was really the man in my life. He was the one who listened to my stories, who cared about my feelings, filling a gap left by George. I had great empathy for George. I did. But he wasn't the only one in this house who had lost their parents.

I was planning to take Imari and Andrea to the zoo that day. On the way, while picking up a few snacks at the drug store, I'd grab a pregnancy test. This was the '80s and while they had made some advancements, this test would take thirty minutes and would clearly show blue if I was indeed pregnant. I was so glad to have Andrea along with us today. I had such a hard time being present that day, but they had each other to entertain themselves.

Mary and I had started to get really close over the past several weeks. I would pop over sometimes while the kids were at school and help her around the house. She seemed to be starved for adult conversation. Hell, I was too. If I'm pregnant, she'd be the only person I'd want to tell. The idea of telling George was stressing me out. But Mary, she would be so happy for me. We'd both have young ones. Maybe they'd grow up to be friends just like their older siblings. The idea of that brought a smile to my face.

I made sure we were back home by 4:00 p.m. so that I could take the test without worrying about George seeing what I was doing. How would he react if he knew we were having another child? Would he descend further into his isolation and resentment of me? Or would this break him out of it? I felt like I knew the answer.

I opened the box and spread out the instructions on the counter in the bathroom. They seemed simple enough—pee on the stick and wait. So, I did. I made note of the time and left the test on the counter, confident that Imari would not enter my room without my permission. He was such a well-behaved, obedient child. He definitely didn't get that from me or his father—the rule breakers that we were. Before I knew it, I was back there on that bench—smelling his cologne...

I was busying myself in the kitchen when I hit the thirty-minute mark. I dropped what I was doing and rushed towards the bedroom. Oh god, what if? I pushed open the door to the bathroom and there it was. I couldn't believe what I was seeing. Blue. I sat on the toilet, holding the plastic stick. Another moment in my life—changed forever in a few minutes. Another baby. I couldn't believe this. How would George react? How would Imari?

I think I understood what would happen with George. He would not be happy about this. He might even insist that I have an abortion. Maybe I just wouldn't tell him until it was too late. No. I couldn't do that. I needed to go to the doctor as soon as possible to confirm this and there was no doing that without getting my hands on that insurance card. If I went behind his back and got the card, he would still find out. All the insurance bills were mailed to him. I could try to intercept it but what if it came on a Saturday when I was out with Imari? It was too risky. I'd have to tell him tonight.

It was that night when we were getting into bed that I told him. I wanted to just see if maybe this could be something he could be happy about. I found an old box that I had that held a necklace that George had bought me back when he did things like that and placed the test in the box and left it on his pillow.

"What is this?" George said, looking only slightly amused.

"Open it."

When he did, I saw the color drain from his face, and I knew I had been right all along.

"You—you can't be."

"Maybe I'm not. I should go to the doctor to be sure."

"These things can be wrong."

"The new tests are very accurate."

"Look. We're comfortable now. I know I probably don't spend enough time with you or do the things I should to make you happy but you can't substitute me with a new baby."

"There's no point talking about this anymore until we're sure. Will you leave me the insurance card so I can make an appointment to see the doctor?"

"And how much is that going to cost? I'm not made of money, you know?"

"Yes. I know. You remind me often. But isn't it better to know the truth as early as possible?" At this he seemed to understand that I was right. If he was going to have any chance of convincing me to have an abortion, we'd have to know if I was truly pregnant as soon as possible.

"Fine." He reached over to his side table, reached into his wallet, and pulled out the card. "Let me know when your appointment is."

"Yes. Of course."

I called the next morning. It was a Friday, and I was lucky. They had a cancelation and could see me in thirty minutes if I could get there. I asked the Antenellis to watch Imari because I had an appointment I needed to rush to, and they were happy to oblige.

I nervously pulled out of the neighborhood and headed across town to the doctor. I couldn't stop myself from imagining the life inside of me—maybe a girl this time. How amazing would that be? And Imari would step up. I know he would. He'd be an amazing older brother filled with love and compassion.

I checked in using the insurance card and paid the $50 copay using George's credit card. I scanned the room and kept landing on families with small children. Was I ready to do this all over again? So much had changed since the '70s when I had Imari. We'd long since thrown out all of Imari's baby things, convinced we were done having children. It was going to be a battle with George to keep this baby. I knew it. But I was determined to win.

8

IMARI

Soon summer was upon us. I didn't know it at the time, but this summer was going to be a very significant one for me. While I had always looked forward to the summers because it meant it was time for more adventures with my mom and the Voyageur, this summer was different. I had a new friend now and my mom definitely took notice and seemed to take a slight step back—encouraging me to step out on my own and go on new adventures with Andrea and any more friends I might make along the way. She had said it would happen but at the time I couldn't imagine wanting to spend time with anyone as much as my mom.

Andrea's parents didn't really seem to mind if Andrea stayed outside all day or mind her hanging out at my house as long as she made it home as soon as the streetlights turned on which, in the summer, happened around 8:00 p.m. Andrea would come down to my house after she'd had breakfast and see if I was awake yet. I always was. I was in the habit of waking up early to have breakfast with my mom, so I was normally up between 7:45 a.m. and 8:30 a.m. We would be having breakfast when Andrea would knock on the front door. Some days, Mom would let me sit in the living room with my cereal and watch cartoons. I had made the transition from Lucky Charms to Corn Pops that summer—much more grown up for a soon-to-be fifth grader. Andrea would come in and join me while I was finishing my breakfast or talking to my mom in the kitchen.

"What's the plan for today, you two?" Mom would always ask. We'd look at each other searching for ideas and then, inevitably, turn to my mom. She'd tell us about some event they were having at the library or about the half-priced tickets for the zoo. We'd load up in the Voyageur and head out. Mom would always stop by Andrea's house and ask to speak to her mom to make sure Andrea had her permission. This always made Andrea worry and me too, if I'm honest. We were worried that somehow my mom would let it slip that Andrea had been riding to school with us every morning and we'd both get in trouble. Invariably, Andrea's mom would appear disheveled at the door with Jeremy on her hip and say it was fine. She would sometimes grab her purse and give Andrea money or offer some to my mom. If we were in a hurry, my mom would often just refuse and tell Andrea's mom that she could pay her some other time.

And it went that way for weeks until things started to change. It all began when I started to wake up before my mom. I was strictly forbidden from entering my parents' bedroom but on that first day when I was awake before my mom, I had walked into the kitchen expecting to see her busying about making breakfast or preparing a packed lunch for me and Andrea for an adventure. This morning, however, when I entered the kitchen, she wasn't there. My father's coffee cup was in the sink as well as the bowl he used to eat his oatmeal—now crusted like stucco on the side of the bowl because, of course, he never cleaned the bowl for himself or even do my mom the courtesy of soaking it in water. Quietly, I walked back down the long hallway to the bedrooms and made my way to my parents' room and knocked gently on the door.

"Mom...Mom, are you awake?" I didn't hear anything in response.

I knocked again but this time a little harder.

"Mom?"

This time I slowly opened the door and went into the room to find my mother still in bed. Terror started to rise in me. I wasn't supposed to be in here but it wasn't like my mom to still be in bed. I approached tentatively and touched my mom on the shoulder.

"Mom?" I said, shaking her slightly. "Mom?"

At this she jerked awake—eyes wide open—startled to see me there.

"Oh my god! Imari? Honey, what are you doing in here? What time is it?"

Looking at my Casio, I said, "It's 8:45, Mom. Are you feeling ok?"

Now fully awake and aware of the fear she saw in my face, she pulled herself up the bed and put a large smile on her face.

"I'm fine, baby. Just a little tired is all. You go in the kitchen now and make yourself a bowl of cereal, ok? I'll be out there shortly."

"Yes ma'am."

When she finally made it to the kitchen, she found me at the kitchen table, nervously eating my cereal. She noticed my demeanor and asked, "What's wrong, baby? You don't need to worry about me. I just over-slept. Parents get tired sometimes too." This did little to change my mood. "Talk to me, baby. What's wrong?"

"Ummm," I started. "I'm sorry I went into your room, Mom. I just wanted to make sure you were ok."

This seemed to relax my mom who was showing real concern at the worry she noticed emanating from me.

"Oh, baby. That's ok. In those situations, you are

allowed in our room. Ok?"

"Ok."

But over the next few weeks of summer, my mom had more moments where she slept in. Andrea said to me, "Maybe you should just let her sleep. She's obviously tired. My dad says if my mom or Jeffrey are ever asleep to just leave them alone."

I considered this and decided she was right. My mom did everything around the house and my dad did nothing but complain. I'd want to sleep in every day too if I was my mom. So, Andrea would come down and I'd have my breakfast in front of the TV, watching Bugs Bunny reruns, and then we'd go outside and explore. Sometimes we'd make sandwiches and bring cookies and have a picnic outside.

One evening on a particularly warm and humid night, I was in my room getting ready for bed when I walked across the hall to the bathroom. There was one bathroom for the entire house. I was stopped in my tracks when I overheard my mom and dad talking in their bedroom with the door slightly open. My mom seemed to be crying or on the verge of tears and my dad appeared to be trying to console her. It was weird to hear my dad talk this way to my mom. It was not something I'd ever heard before. I edged myself closer so I could hear.

"Look. There's no need worrying about it before

we have all the test results in. You're a young, healthy woman. You heard what the doctor said. There's no reason to panic yet."

Without noticing it, I was inching closer and closer when I heard the floorboard squeak beneath my foot. At this, I turned quickly and dashed into the bathroom. Had they heard me?

I sat down on the toilet with thoughts rushing through my head. What had I just heard? The acid in my stomach started to rise and my mouth started to water. *Oh god,* I thought, *I'm going to throw up.* Just then there were two loud bangs on the bathroom door.

"Boy! You better be brushin' yo teeth in there! I want you in bed in five minutes," exclaimed my father.

"Yes sir."

I slowly got up from the toilet, willing the contents of my stomach to stay put. I brushed my teeth quickly and got in bed under the safety of my blanket—hugging one of my pillows as tightly as I could. The earth beneath me seemed unstable, wavy, so I clung even more tightly to the pillow until my arms started to hurt.

Suddenly, I realized I was not alone anymore and tentatively peeked my head out from under the blankets while still holding my pillow with one arm.

There I saw my mom looking at me—eyes red like she had been crying. She was watching me—waiting on me to break the silence.

"Mom, have you been crying?"

I could see the wheels turning in her head. She had a choice to make in that moment: would she lie to me and try to keep me shielded from what was going on or tell me the truth and completely upend my life forever?

"I'm sick, baby."

"Sick?" I was somewhat relieved by this. I could be a bit of a baby when I got sick too. But it only really lasted for a few days and I would get better.

"Yes."

"Like a cold?"

"No, baby. Not like a cold."

"Then what? Are you going to be ok?"

"Sweetie, I don't know." Still, she was hesitating—considering how much to tell me. Suddenly, she seemed resolved to tell it all to me. As she talked, I sat up in my bed and tried to hold on to every word but the earth started to move again or was I the one moving? Was I shaking? I couldn't really understand everything she was saying. I was startled when I realized I was crying. I was no longer connected to my body. I was hovering outside of myself, watching the untethering of this poor boy—learning in real-time the power of words and how, in a few seconds, they have the power to destroy your life.

It wasn't until she touched my hand that I was drawn back into my body. My eyes, however, could not rise to meet my mother's gaze.

"I know this is a lot to take in, baby. Do you have any questions?"

Still staring down at my blanket, I asked, "Are you going to die?"

"Baby. No one gets out of this world alive. We are all going to die. When things like this happen, we can either bury our heads in the sand and pretend it isn't happening or we can use it to remind us of how precious life is and how we should live each day as if it is our last. Because one day, it will be."

IMANI

It feels like a lifetime ago when I was on my way to the doctor to confirm my pregnancy when in fact it has only been a few weeks. My primary doctor was able to confirm my pregnancy and shuffled me off to an OB/GYN, an old white man whose face read like a history of the world, deep lines telling the story of many moms to be. Dr. Matheny gave me an outline of what needed to happen over the next few weeks. He had been the doctor who had told me that I would not likely ever conceive due to the overwhelming number of cyst in my ovaries caused by an underlying condition. He'd said there were procedures—none of them covered by our insurance so we'd decided, George and I, that Imari would be our only child.

Dr. Matheny wanted to do an examination to see how things were going. I was already fifteen weeks along. I thought maybe I'd lie to George and say I was further along. I knew there was no way I was going to let George talk me into terminating this child—my miracle baby.

Small moments change your life forever. I saw it on the doctor's face. He wanted to do some more tests.

"Why? Is something wrong?"

I asked but I knew, didn't I? I had for years now felt like I was constantly paying for my original sin, having sex before marriage. The voice of my mother in my head echoed. "Girl. You'll see. You'll provoke the vengeance of God and there will be no amount of prayer that will save you." She was right and here it was—a prophecy made true. Some abnormalities. More test needed. Decisions to be made.

My visit to the doctor had taken much longer than I had expected. By the time I had stopped to pick up some dinner and grab Imari from the Antenellis, George was already home from work. We ate at the kitchen table in near silence. It was always a careful dance at the kitchen table. I knew better than to ask Imari about his day with the Antenellis. It would provoke all manner of judgment from George and send Imari deeper into his shell. But I had no energy left to devote to this today. Despite my worry, I was ravenous. I'd cleared my plate and part of Imari's. The baby. She was hungry. There had been no confirmation of the sex, but I knew. She was a girl because that's what I wanted and why I knew I must lose her. Vengeance.

It wasn't until bedtime, when Imari was brushing his teeth for bed, that I told George everything the doctor had said. The concern in his eyes. All that he had suspected. His referral to oncology. George was concerned. He'd never considered that he might lose me before that and I was back to that moment, the last chance we had to be happy right before his parents died. He was hugging me and telling me that everything would be ok. That there were more tests that needed to happen. I allowed myself to lean into him. To hope. We were interrupted by that creak in the floor that we both knew all too well. Imari had heard our conversation.

When I went into his room to confirm what he'd heard, I didn't have to ask one question. He was under the safety of his blanket and when he noticed I was there, it was all over his face. Terror. There were so many times in my life when I was a child that my parents had lied to me—small lies meant to keep me in line or keep me in the dark. How many of us do this? We see a fault in our parents, in the way they have raised us, and we vow not to do the same with our own children. This was one of those moments. I had decided then to tell him the truth but how much should I tell him? I'd only tell him that I was sick and that the doctor was worried.

"I know we haven't talked much about the parts of the reproductive system or even what that means but there are parts that women are born with that men don't have that all work together to make a baby."

Imari stared at me, still gripped by fear.

"Have you heard of cancer?"

Imari nodded.

"Well, I'm still doing tests, but the doctor believes my reproductive parts have cancer in them and is worried that it may have spread to other parts of my body."

When we were done talking and I'd finally put him to bed, I could tell I had done nothing to alleviate his worries. What a nightmare this must be for him. When I closed the door to his room, George was there.

"Do you really think it was wise to be that honest with him?"

"I don't know."

"How did he take it?"

"Oh, honey. As well as a nine-year old could, I guess. I'm sure he's devastated."

"Well, it's done now. At least you don't have to worry about hiding it from him. You didn't tell him you were pregnant, I noticed."

"Yeah. I felt like that was too much to add to his plate when we don't even know yet what's going to happen to her."

"Her?"

"It's just a feeling."

9

IMARI

The next morning, I woke up to the sun streaming through the curtains in my room. They were dinosaur curtains—a remnant from when I was four and could talk of nothing but dinosaurs. I rubbed my eyes and swung my legs over the side of the bed. They seemed particularly heavy this morning. I reached up to the sky in a yawn and went to stand. It was then that I remembered the conversation with my mom that night and collapsed back down on to the bed. I eased myself back into bed. I thought, *Maybe if I stay in bed long enough, I just won't have to face this new reality.* I could hear my mother moving around the house—minding her daily chores. The washer was going. I smelled bacon and pancakes maybe. My growling stomach started to overcome my will to

avoid the day but I fought against it—grabbing my
trusty pillow that had borne the weight of my despair last night, pulling it into my stomach. I heard a
knock at the door—Andrea. I listened to their mum-
bled voices through the walls of my room and then
heard the door close. I definitely was not in the mood
to entertain Andrea's energy today.

Curiosity finally got the better of me and I pulled
myself out of bed and made it sloppily. As I entered
the kitchen, my mom was there in blue jeans and a
sleeveless shirt. She had put on some makeup and
her hair was tied neatly back in a French braid.

"Where's Andrea?"

"I told her we needed to spend some time alone
together today."

At this, I met my mother's eyes and I saw all the
warmth I always saw when I looked into her eyes.

Stealing her line, I said, "So what's the plan for
today?"

"We haven't been to our pond in a while. Let's go
say hello to our ducks. I fear they have been missing
our treats."

I quickly finished my breakfast and rinsed my dish
and glass and placed them in the sink to be washed
later.

My mom grabbed her bag of bread, already torn
into pieces, and we headed out the front door and

down the driveway—the way we had so many times in the past. We traversed the path and made it to the duck pond. Today though, the ducks were there waiting on us. How did they know?

We sat there in the sun with a small breeze off the lake filling the air with the scent of the lilies. And my mom told stories just like she used to, of warriors and princesses, of kings and peasants, of love and loss. As she told these stories, I watched the ducks, knowing they were pedaling so furiously under the water yet looking so serene, gliding across the top. Somehow, this seemed to resonate with me. When we were finished at the pond, we jumped inside the Voyageur. My mom slid open the glass window.

"Where to, Prince Imari?"

"To the yogurt place!"

"TCBY? Yes. Of course, my prince."

We had our yogurts while walking through the mall. I saw a few friends from school. I waved at them with no intention of stopping to talk to them but my mom said she needed to run into one of the women's clothing stores and that I should stay and talk to my friends. Disappointed, I agreed.

"Hey look. It's e-mommy. Who hangs out with their mommy at the mall?" one of the boys said.

"Yeah. So lame. What a momma's boy!" another exclaimed.

A rage set fire within me and before I knew it, my

mom was there pulling me off both of the boys.

"Enough!" my mother said to me. "Enough."

Back in the car, I explained to my mom what the boys had said and how angry it had made me.

"Baby. It's ok to be angry. Kids can be cruel. But it's never ok for violence to be your first response. You're going to need to learn how to stand up for yourself with your words."

I thought about how my cousin Monica had so quickly put Bruce in his place in school. I considered this and nodded my head.

"I'm sorry, Mom. We were having such a good day."

"Baby, we still are. You don't have to let the bumps in the road determine your entire day. If you learn from your mistakes, then you've made the most of it. It's the best way to learn really."

Over the next couple of weeks, my mom started to teach me so much: how to do laundry, how to cook breakfast, how to properly wash dishes and make my bed, when to take out the garbage and set the alarm clock. Then she let me try them all, correcting my mistakes in the moment. The best lesson though, by far, was the day my mom taught me how to drive. I had to sit on a few phone books to see above the steering wheel but my legs were long enough already to reach the pedals. We were in a vacant parking lot and I couldn't believe this was happening.

"Now first, Imari, you must check your mirrors. There are three of them. You want to have a complete picture of what's going on around you. It's not enough to just stay in your lane though this is also very important," she said as she nudged me and I laughed, excited.

We spent the day driving, parking, and changing imaginary lanes. At the end of the day, Mom turned to me and said, "You're a natural!"

These had been such an exciting few weeks even though I knew why mom was in such a hurry to impart as much knowledge as she could. We never talked about it though. And every day, my mom made an effort to get out of bed before me, shower, and get dressed. She would do her hair and put on makeup. When I would join her in the kitchen, she already had the day planned out and I was always so excited. What would I learn today?

We went on that way through the end of the summer. Andrea had spent her last few weeks of summer at some Christian camp. But today was the first day of fifth grade and she was here at my doorstep. As she entered, she gave me a big hug.

"Imari! I missed you! I want to hear all about your summer. Mine was pretty dull but I did meet some new people, which was good. One of them lives on the other side of this neighborhood. I'm hoping we can all be good friends. Her name is Angie. Do you know her?

"No." I was feeling something strange as Andrea described this girl. What was it?

"So, tell me about your summer. Did you go on many adventures with your mom?"

Before I could answer, my mom came into the room and ushered us back to the kitchen. As she had done with me, Andrea ran up to my mom and gave her a big hug and started to talk about her summer. For a moment, all was right with the world, and I smiled to myself thinking, *What if things could just be like they were?*

IMANI

I was eighteen years old when I had Imari and in a lot of ways, we grew up together. He was in my thoughts so much these days. My test results had come back. The cancer had started in my ovaries but had spread everywhere—aggressively taking over the healthy cells in my body, the way a bad smell cuts through a room, lingering. Stage IV. My chances of survival were small. Perhaps if I had taken care of the cysts in my ovaries when I was eighteen.... The doctor said my best shot at survival was to abort my child and start chemo immediately, followed by a course of radiation. Not just an abortion though—a full hysterectomy. George had pleaded with me to listen to reason, but I could not sacrifice the life of my daughter to save my own. I wouldn't do it.

I understood what this meant. I was likely sealing both of our fates—mine and my unborn child—but my chances of survival were small anyway. No. I would just try to survive long enough to carry my daughter to term and then I would start chemo. I had wondered in the back of my mind why George wanted me to abort her. Was he really worried about my survival or was he selfishly concerned about having another mouth to feed? He'd also thought I should let my parents know. It's not like I didn't think about my parents all the time and of course I thought about them when I found out this news. It had been ten years now since we had spoken. George was right though. They did deserve to know.

"Hello?"

"Hi Mom."

"Ingrid, sweetheart? Is that you?" For a moment, I held on to that feeling—what it felt like to hear my mom call me "sweetheart."

"No, Mom. It's me. Imani."

"Oh. Girl. I told you. You made your decision and what that meant. What are you calling here for now? Money, I'm guessing."

That stung and made me angry. I wanted to respond in a way to knock the wind out of her. "I'm dying."

"You're—you're what?"

"Cancer. And it's spread all over my body. And I'm pregnant."

"My Lord in heaven."

"I just thought you should know."

"Imani—"

I hung up. I don't know what she was going to say but I was not going to give her the satisfaction of saying what I knew she would. I already had her voice in my head. I didn't need to hear it out loud. "This is God's punishment." No. She didn't deserve the chance to say that.

The next morning, I made sure to wake early. I had been sleeping in a lot lately and I could see how it was worrying Imari. The summer had started, and this was our time together—maybe our last time alone together before the baby arrived. I had not told him about the baby yet. I didn't want to confuse him. Maybe he'd think I was dying because of the baby. No. She was blameless in all this and if I did die after she was born, I needed Imari to understand that it wasn't because of her. While I was thinking this, I felt her move! God, it had been so long since I felt that feeling—a life growing inside of me. I had just hit week sixteen so this was all normal. Was it possible that I'd actually have a healthy baby?

Soon, we'd have to start cleaning out the back bedroom that we'd been using as storage and a second closet. The room was in the back corner of the house and got really good light. She'd love it here. I was envisioning the room—yellow maybe. But I couldn't dream for long. I had been having sharp pains the past couple of days and I was feeling one then. Was it the cancer or was there something wrong with the baby?

I couldn't talk to George about any of this. I knew that George loved me. I could see the concern in his face when he would look at me now. He still wanted me to abort the baby but we were getting close to when that would no longer be an option. Because of this though, I couldn't really share what was going on with me and the baby. He wanted no part in it.

I did need to confide in someone and the only person to come to mind was Mary.

While she knew I had been going to doctor appointments, she did not know anything else. On one of these days, I decided I'd drop Imari off early at the Antenellis and asked Mary if she had a few moments where we could chat in private. We made our way to the kitchen. She placed Jeffrey in his highchair and spread some cereal out in front of him.

"Can I get you tea or coffee?"

"Just a glass of water for me."

Mary walked over to grab the water. It was always interesting to see how other moms navigated their kitchens—almost on auto pilot, grabbing the cup from the cabinet, the water from the fridge, checking on Jeffrey before landing in front of me with my water at the kitchen table.

"Mary, I was just wondering if I could talk to you about what's going on with me."

"Oh. I hope everything is ok?"

"Well..."

And I launched into it. Once I started talking, I couldn't stop. I told her everything—the cancer, the baby, the pains I was having, how George wanted me to have an abortion. When I was finished, I noticed that at some point in the conversation, Mary had reached over to hold my hand with both of hers. When had that happened? She was still holding it now as her eyes filled with tears. She temporarily removed one hand to wipe her eyes before grabbing my hand again.

"First, Imani, I'm so glad you shared that with me. It must be a relief to let some of that out."

"Yes. Yes, it is."

"Second, you need to go to the doctor and tell him about the pains you're having."

"Actually, I'm headed there this morning. I just wanted to talk to you first. I needed someone to know everything that was going on."

"Well, please let me know if you need anything at all."

"You're already doing a lot. Just having someone to talk to and to watch after Imari is such a relief. I can't begin to tell you."

"Of course. Well, I'm here if you need anything else. Anything at all."

"Thanks, Mary."

"You're welcome." At this we both stood, and Mary pulled me into a big hug. I'd forgotten what this felt like—to be held by someone my size. I could feel myself starting to crumble and quickly pulled away.

"I should be back by 1:00 o'clock."

"Take your time. Don't worry about Imari. I've got him."

At that, I was out the door on my way to the appointment. I had another sharp pain. And then another. Something was wrong. By the time I made it to the doctor, I was doubled over in pain. I eased my way out of the truck and made my way towards the front of the doctor's office, only one block away from the main hospital. As I made it through the doors, the woman at the first desk noticed I was in pain and yelled for the doctor.

"Doctor Phillips! Please hurry!"

Soon they were both at my side, putting me in a wheelchair.

"Imari, listen. You're in some distress. We need to get you over to the ER. We're just going to wheel you over, ok?" Dr. Phillips sounded unreasonably calm.

"Ok," I said, barely able to get the word out of my mouth.

As they pushed me the one block over to the emergency room, I held on tight to the arm of the wheelchair with one hand and gripped my stomach with the other—breathing short shallow breaths, sweat beading on my brow. People on the sidewalk gave us a large berth as we passed—understanding the situation and showing looks of deep concern. I was concerned too. The doctor had tried to mask it, but he was worried as well. I could see his thoughts written on his face. *I'm losing her.*

They immediately placed me on a gurney and wheeled me back and then my legs were in stirrups. There were a few nurses in the room—one connecting me to an IV, attaching things to me. I felt like an appliance with all the wires and tubes coming out of me. In between the shooting pain, I would try to gauge the situation by looking in their eyes. They were a giveaway. They had clearly been taught not to show concern on their faces, but their eyes could not lie. We, my daughter and I, were in trouble.

At that moment, I heard a commotion just outside the door to the room.

"That's my damn wife in there. You have to let me in!" yelled George.

"Please. Can I see him?"

"Nurse, let him in. Just for a few seconds, ok, Mrs. Johnson?" Dr. Phillips said.

"Yes. Ok."

George pushed past the nurse to rush to my side.

"Baby. What's going on?"

The doctor interjected. "Mr. Johnson, your wife and child are in distress. We're connecting the fetal monitor now to check on the baby."

"What do you mean, 'in distress'? Are they going to be ok?"

Before the doctor could answer, the ultrasound tech whispered something in the doctor's ear.

"What's wrong?" I said.

"Mrs. Johnson. I'm so sorry but we cannot find the baby's heartbeat."

"What? Keep trying," I said, tears flooding my eyes—I gripped George's hand tightly and he squeezed back, letting me know he was there.

"I'm so sorry. But you are still in distress. Your heartrate is very high. We've given you medication to bring your heartrate down but you're in labor."

"Oh god," George said. Realizing the scene that was about to play out in front of both of us.

"Doctor. Can George please stay? I don't want to go through this alone."

"Yes. But George, if anything starts to jeopardize your wife, we're going to need you to step out of the room. Clear?"

"Yes. I understand," George said solemnly. I could tell what he was thinking. He was going to lose both of us. God, I hoped he was wrong.

10

IMARI

A new schoolyear meant a new homeroom teacher. This year, for fifth grade, we had Mr. Smith—my first male homeroom teacher. He wasn't at all warm like Ms. Jenkins. He made us sit alphabetically which meant Andrea and I weren't sitting together this year. As he called Andrea's name to sit in the first desk, she looked at me and frowned and made her way to her new desk for the year. I ended up a row over in the back. Unfortunately, that put me right behind Bruce Jackson—who was notorious for causing trouble and cheating off his neighbors. He was also the one who had come up with my nickname "Momma's Boy." I think he was a little upset to not have thought of my new nickname, "E-mommy." Imari, E-mommy—it was sort of sitting right there.

That had been LeDarius. Of course, Bruce wasn't much of a creative person. I was actually surprised to see him here in the fifth grade, given that he could barely read.

"I get to sit next to E-mommy," Bruce said through his laughter.

"No talking back there," said Mr. Smith. "I don't want to hear any talking unless I ask you to speak. Do you understand, Bruce and Imari?"

"Yes sir," I said quickly.

Bruce rolled his eyes and turned around. He was already getting us in trouble. This was going to be a long school year.

As we switched classes to go to English (we only had Mr. Smith for Math and Science), we had to line up—again alphabetically. Mr. Smith marched us like a military platoon heading into war to Mrs. Hunt's class. Immediately, the energy had changed.

"Hello! My new fifth graders! We're going to have so much fun this year. Pick any seat you want but pick carefully, you'll be in that seat for the rest of the year."

I quickly found Andrea and we waited until Bruce and LeDarius had picked their seats in the back. We chose seats on the opposite side of the room near the front.

"Ugh. It sucks that you have to sit next to Bruce. I got to sit next to Angie. Angie Blackburn. You remember I told you about her. She was at church camp. Of course, it doesn't matter since we aren't able to make a sound in old man Smith's class. He's so mean. And man, does his breath stink! I think he smokes. Yuck!"

"I'd rather deal with bad breath than have to sit next to Bruce."

"Yeah. You're right."

"Have a seat everyone. I'm sending around a sheet that has all the desks on it. Please put your name down for the desk you're sitting in. Last chance to move," Mrs. Hunt said, looking slyly around at the class.

As Mrs. Hunt went through the plan for the school year, it was clear that we were in store for a great year. She had wonderfully thought-out plans and creative projects. This year, we were going to be learning about poetry. She then reached to her desk and picked up a book with a black and white cover. Already, this was vastly different from the English books in fourth grade that were filled with color.

"Boys and girls, this book of poems is entitled Where the Sidewalk Ends by Shel Silverstein." Then she began to read. Andrea and I were on the edge our seats immediately as Mrs. Hunt began to read a descriptive poem about a girl who eats a whale. I'd never heard anything like it before. And when she finished, we all, nearly in unison, called out for another.

"Ok. Just one more," she said, looking through the tops of her glasses that she would put on to read but otherwise would hang on a gold chain around her neck.

By the end of her class, it was time for lunch so we made our way, single file, to the lunchroom. I couldn't get those poems out of my head. I had no idea that words could be used in such a way before—to create such wonderfully weird worlds that stretched my imagination and concept of what was possible. These thoughts were immediately interrupted as I lost my footing and fell hard onto the hard floor of the cafeteria in front of the entire school. It wasn't until I heard Bruce and LeDarius laughing that I understood that I had been tripped.

"Awww. Are you gonna cry, little momma's boy?"

Andrea was immediately at my side, pulling me off the floor.

"Why don't you leave him alone?"

"Are you gonna tell on me, church girl?"

"Yeah. Maybe I will!"

Too embarrassed to engage in this, I grabbed my lunch tray and got into line. This year, my mom had decided it was probably best that I eat school lunch instead of bringing lunch from home. She tried to spin it as being more grown up, but I knew it was really because she was just too tired to make it. In fact, she had gotten too tired to make dinner as well. This meant that my dad had to make dinner most nights, which usually meant fast food. I was actually fine with this and with the school lunch—especially on pizza Fridays.

Another change was coming and I knew it. She was going to have to stop driving me and Andrea to school. I was dreading this because Bruce and LeDarius rode the same bus—though they didn't live in the same neighborhood. When the day finally came just a few days after the start of the new school year, I tried to pretend like it wasn't a big deal because I could see how pained it made my mom to have to admit that she couldn't take us anymore.

The first morning of our new bus-riding adventure, Andrea and I climbed on the bus. Right at the front, near the bus driver, sat Andrea's friend Angie. She had saved a spot for Andrea.

"Andrea. I have a space here!"

Andrea looked at me, searching. I said, "It's ok. Go ahead. I'll find a seat."

Of course, the only seats were in the back near Bruce and LeDarius.

"What's up, E-mommy? Did yo mommy pack you a bottle and your blanky?" They all laughed like it was the funniest thing they'd ever heard. I sat down next to a chubby boy named Chris who seemed to be happy there was someone else there to divert some of the attention from Bruce.

"Chris. Take his bag to see what what his mommy

brought him."

Chris looked sheepishly up at me and under his breath said, "Sorry," as he snatched my bag away from me and tossed it back to Bruce. Bruce grabbed the bag and started riffling through it—throwing my papers and notebooks on the ground.

"Nope. No bottle," he laughed as he watched me scurry around picking up the paper. I grabbed my bag back from him and he didn't resist. He'd had his fun. I got back to my seat and tried to reorganize my papers. I stole a glance to the front of the bus to see if Andrea had seen but she was too engrossed in her conversation with Angie to have noticed.

As we got off, I quickly rushed ahead to homeroom and to my desk. At least I knew for homeroom, math, and science, I wouldn't have to worry about Bruce laughing at me. In fact, I got the opportunity to watch him struggle when getting called to the board to read aloud, which made me feel something. I wasn't happy and I didn't really think it was funny. It simply felt like the sweet satisfaction of revenge.

IMANI

Labor lasted for twelve hours. It was agony—working so hard to deliver my girl when I knew she was already gone. There was a part of me though that hoped they were wrong. That I would deliver her and would hear her cry. But at the end of the twelve hours, my hope was shattered. They let me hold her. She was tiny of course but she looked like a baby—tiny little head, arms, and legs—all fit in the palm of my hand. Her name would have been Destiny, I had decided. It just felt appropriate given all the large life-defining moments that were happening.

George had arranged for Imari to spend the night with the Antenellis. He had school in the morning. The doctors wanted to keep me for a couple of days just to monitor my heartrate but George and I both decided it was time to go home after the one night. I needed to get back home to my little man. We'd decided not to tell him about the baby. It was all just too much for him, we thought—losing a sister, maybe losing his mom. George wanted me to see the oncologist right away. We didn't need to delay the chemo any longer now that we'd lost Destiny. He wanted me to fight but I felt gut punched. My beautiful little girl—gone. My mother's voice in my head. I shook my head violently. No! I wasn't giving my mother any more space in my head. And I would fight. I'd fight for the men in my life who still needed me.

That next day, I started chemo. I'd seen women going through chemo in movies, but I had not personally known anyone who had gone through it. They had listed out all of the side effects from the chemo: hair loss, fatigue, decreased ability to fight infections. But no one mentioned the smell. I stank.

I could smell it seeping out of my pores and it made me nauseous.

The Antenellis were a godsend—especially Mary. George had to keep working so Mary would go with me to chemo along with little Jeffrey, full of life. Sometimes Jeffrey would sit on my lap, and I'd read to him. It was a welcome distraction. I cherished these times actually. It felt amazing to have the support of a friend, another mother who understood everything that was going on in my head—the fear of losing my life and the fear of not being around for my son and husband.

It was during one of these sessions that I decided I needed to ask something of Mary to give me some peace of mind. It was a large ask and I wasn't sure what she would say.

"Mary, I was wondering if I could talk to you about something."

"Yes, of course."

"It's been so amazing getting to know you these past couple of months. I've loved getting to spend our afternoons together long before I was sick. It's been lovely having a friend. It's been so long it feels like since I've had one. My only regret was that I didn't get a chance to know you sooner. What you have done for our family, we can never repay you."

"Oh, it's nothing, Imani. Really. We love Imari like he was our own. He's been such a great influence on Andrea."

At this, I felt my throat catch and tears starting to form in my eyes.

"Thank you for saying that, Mary. It makes what I'm about to ask you so much easier." I took a deep breath. "Mary, you know I love George, but he doesn't have the skills or the desire to raise my son—not in the way he needs." I reached into my purse and handed her an envelope.

"What's this?"

"It's my final wishes regarding Imari. I know you don't really know me that well but I believe you when you say you love my son. And I know, and this is so hard to say, that you love my son more than his own father does."

"I'm sure that's not—"

"It's true, Mary. Mary, in this envelope is a letter outlining how I want Imari raised and who I want him raised by. If you and Andrew are willing, I'd like that to be you."

"Oh, Imani," Mary said, holding my hand now—eyes overflowing with tears. "Of course, we will. We'll raise him like our own."

"Don't you need to talk this over with Andrew?"

"Psh! I wear the pants in my house."

At this, we both laughed too hard—a release of tension and pain.

Imari knew that I was getting medicine and that it was going to make me sick before it made me better.

I tried to get up with him in the morning as much as I could and talk to him before he left for school. He had started making his own breakfast in the mornings—a bowl of cereal and a banana and some orange juice. I could tell he didn't want to burden me with things going on at school, but I could tell things weren't going well.

"Are you making any new friends?"

He looked up at me through the tops of his eyes. That look always destroyed me—made me crumble with empathy for my son.

"Umm. I have Andrea. She's like three friends in one."

"That she is," I said, laughing and coughing some. I could see the look of concern in his face. I was concerned too. I had not been feeling well over the past few days. It was likely the chemo but it felt like something else.

"Baby, I know you're worried about me. I'm worried too. But, no matter what happens, you're going to be ok. I don't want you to worry. You know how much I love you, right, baby?"

"Yes, Mom. I love you too," he said—his eyes filled with more worry.

I couldn't send him off to school this way. "Want to have pizza tonight for dinner?"

At this, his eyes lit up. "Can we?"

"Of course, baby. Now, wash out that bowl and your cup and get ready for the bus."

"Yes ma'am."

He did as I asked and grabbed his book bag and headed for the door. At the door, he gave me kiss. He was nearly as tall as I was already. I caressed the side of his face.

"Have a good day, baby, and I'll see you for pizza tonight."

"Ok, Mom. Love you. Bye!"

As soon as he was out the door, I slid down the back of the door, overwhelmed by pain—emotional and physical in equal parts. I sat there for minutes, maybe hours, crying from my depths—that place in you reserved for the darkest moments.

Then I had a vision of me in a white flowing gown. I must be dreaming. I'm walking through the woods along our path towards the pond. I can smell the lilies. Oh! They smell so amazing. I want to stay here forever.

11

IMARI

I have always heard about how unlucky the number thirteen is and how it should be avoided at all costs. I was in an elevator once with my parents in Atlanta when my mom explained why there was no 13th floor. It had all seemed so strange to me at the time. Why would you spend time being afraid of a number when there were so many real-life things to be afraid of: the Albertson's pit bull, getting embarrassed at school, that old abandoned shed just north of the pond. But it was on my 13th day of the school year while in my English class listening to Mrs. Hunt read poetry that my life was changed forever. I knew it was day thirteen because Mrs. Hunt would always welcome us to class by telling us which day of the school year it was:

"Welcome, fifth graders, to day thirteen! Let's make it a magical one!"

The moments leading up to that moment when I was pulled out of class are bit of a blur. Andrea and I were listening intently to the poem being read by Mrs. Hunt and I was trying to imagine myself as the little boy in the tree in the poem when there was a knock on the door.

"Excuse me, students," Mrs. Hunt said as she went to the door.

She stepped away and the kids in the classroom immediately started whispering. I was still deep in thought about the poem when I noticed that Mrs. Hunt was standing next to me.

"Imari, sweetheart. Mrs. Thompson needs to speak with you. Please gather your things, ok?"

A bit confused, I gathered my things and stood to follow Mrs. Hunt back to the door. I looked back quickly at Andrea whose eyes were filled with concern. When our eyes met, she smiled at me. At the door, I looked up at Mrs. Hunt who looked like she was on the verge of tears.

"Please follow Mrs. Thompson, sweetheart."

"Hi Imari. I'm Mrs. Thompson, the school counselor. Would you mind coming with me to my office?"

"Ok," I said. Fear started to well up inside of me and the corners of my vision started to blur.

When we made it to Mrs. Thompson's office, I sat down in the chair in front of her desk. Instead of sitting behind her desk, Mrs. Thompson took the seat beside me and took my hand.

"Oh, dear Imari. I have some really terrible news your father asked me to share with you before he arrives in a few minutes. Your mom passed away this morning. I'm so very sorry."

"No. I was just with her. We're having pizza tonight."

"I'm so sorry. She's gone."

I immediately dissolved into tears and fell into Mrs. Thompson's arms. Soon there were other voices in the room, but I didn't know who they were—other office staff most likely. I just buried my face more deeply in Mrs. Thompson's chest. There was some strange sound, like a wounded animal coming from somewhere in the room. It was moments later that I realized that the noise was coming from me. The others in the room were now crying too. I could hear sniffling noses around me—a symphony of grief, empathy, and sorrow.

I was floating, descending into an unknown swarm of emotion and uncertainty. So much of my life had been about routine and expected outcomes. But now, I had no idea what was coming next and it all happened so fast. How long had it been since Mrs. Thompson ruined my life with nouns and verbs? I couldn't move. Someone was going to have to tell me what to do next. What was I supposed to do now?

I guess my father would have to come get me. He'd have to leave work. Would he even do that? Yes. He didn't care at all about me but I know he loved my mom. There was no denying that.

The next few moments were a blur. Suddenly I was in the front seat of my father's old Cadillac, the cold and cracked leather an appropriate vehicle for my empty soul. We rode in silence back to our house. My head felt too heavy to lift—weighted down by the ever-flowing tears. Could you run out of tears? It certainly didn't seem like I would. A few times, I glanced over at this man to see if he registered any emotions on his face. I was careful not to get caught. I didn't want to engage with him. Not now. It's hard to describe what I saw when I finally caught a glimpse of his face. The best way I could describe it was that the light had gone out.

Back home, I immediately walked to my room and climbed under the covers. Soon there were voices in the kitchen and the clicking and clanking of dishes and silverware. I wasn't really sure if it had been minutes or hours. I think I may have drifted off to sleep at one point. As the noise in the house continued to increase, I would sink further into the bed, gripping my pillow tightly. I was awakened by a small knock on my door. I didn't immediately peek my head out until I heard that recognizable voice.

"Imari?"

"Oh, hi, Andrea."

She came into the room and sat on the corner of the bed.

"I like your room. I have to share a room with Jeffrey. Just for now though. They are going to redo the downstairs and I'll have my own room. My parents will move down there, I think. It'll be a while though."

I was so grateful to just be able to listen and not have to speak. I wasn't sure I could. It had been hours since I even tried.

"Imari, I'm so sorry," Andrea said as her eyes overflowed with tears. "I just don't understand how this could happen. She was so young. She is the same age as my parents. Was the same age...I mean, do you know what happened? Was she sick?"

"Yes. She was sick."

"Oh." Andrea wanted to ask more, and I could see the amount of effort it took her not to.

"Are you hungry? There's so much food out there. Even my mom made something. Some sort of casserole. She's actually a pretty good cook."

"I'm not hungry."

"I'll go get some anyway. Your dad said we could eat here in your room." Not only was Andrea never allowed back to my room, but I was never allowed to eat in here.

Moments later, Andrea returned with two large plates of food and cans of soda in each of her pockets.

I pulled myself from under the covers and joined Andrea on the ground where she had already started to eat—mac and cheese, and ham, and green beans, fried chicken and cornbread. My stomach betrayed me as I heard it growl. Despite myself, I started to eat. I was much hungrier than I had thought.

Andrea filled me in on the rest of the day. She said that Mrs. Hunt couldn't continue with the reading and had the class try writing their own poems about the thing that brought us the most joy. And when the class started to read the poems, Mrs. Hunt started to cry.

"Now I know why she was crying but at the time we all thought it was a strange way to respond to such happy poems. I guess people cry when they're happy too though," Andrea said thoughtfully.

"Of course, Bruce and LeDarius said awful stuff that I'm not gonna say. But most people sensed that something bad was going on and were genuinely worried for you."

I nodded my head, not really wanting to say anything in response to that.

After getting caught up, Andrea pulled down some of the board games I had on my bookcase. We tried a few but they were really designed to be played by more than two people. I think my parents continued to buy them for me in hopes that I would have more than one friend. Well, it was probably my mom really who had done that. I guess I wouldn't have to worry about getting any more board games.

Eventually, we settled on a game my dad had bought me for my last birthday, Battleship.

Hours must have passed. Long enough that I was hungry again. Andrea was too.

"Want me to get us some more food?"

"Yeah," I said—a bit guilty that I was too afraid to leave my room and enter the swarm of voices. I didn't know it then, but it was actually a great decision because over the next few days, I was going to have what felt like hundreds of uncomfortable conversations with strangers offering their condolences to me.

After we ate again and the voices started to thin out, there was a knock at the door. Andrea's mom appeared at the door. For the first time, she didn't have Jeffrey on her hip and her hair was pulled back neatly in a French braid. I hadn't noticed before but she was a very pretty woman. She came in and had a seat on my bed as Andrea and I looked up at her from the floor where we were playing card games.

"Hi, Imari, sweetheart. Have you had enough to eat?"

"Yes ma'am."

"I got us loads of food, Mom."

"Oh, good. And are you doing ok?" She pondered this briefly before continuing. "I'm sure you don't really know. You're going to have a lot of people asking you that over the next few days and weeks. It's ok if you don't have an answer."

Before I knew it, I was crying again. Mrs. Antenelli knelt down and scooped me up in her arms. She smelled wonderful—floral. It reminded me of the lake and the lilies and of my mother. Soon, Andrea was hugging me too.

After a few moments, Mrs. Antenelli stood and said to Andrea, "We should be leaving soon."

"Oh, Mom. Can't I stay a little longer?"

I looked up from the ground directly at Mrs. Antenelli. She must have seen the pleading in my eyes. "Stay here for a moment, Andrea, while I have a chat with your father."

"Ok!"

As soon as she left the room, Andrea turned to me.

"Sorry my mom made you cry. She really does mean well."

"Oh, I know. It's ok."

We returned to our card games as we waited on Andrea's mom to return. When she did, she asked Andrea to step out for a minute so she could chat with her but assured me that she would be right back. Seconds later, I heard Andrea exclaim, "Really, Mom? Oh, thank you!"

"Shhh! Quiet, honey," she said in response.

Back at my door, Mrs. Antenelli spoke. "Imari, dear. If it's ok with you, Andrea's going to spend the night here with you. I've already spoken it over with your father. Andrea's dad has already gone to get

Andrea's sleeping bag. Your dad said you have one too in your closet," she said as she stepped into my room and opened my closet.

"Yes, ma'am," I said, getting to my feet and heading over to the closet to assist. "It's just there on the top shelf."

She reached up and pulled the sleeping bag down.

"Andrea will stay here tonight and, in the morning, I'll come get you both for breakfast. Then, Imari dear, you're going to stay with us tomorrow and Friday. Your dad has to get the arrangements in order for your mom's memorial, which will be on Sunday. We're going to have Andrea stay home from school with you tomorrow and Friday too. How does that sound, Imari?"

I was smiling ear to ear. "Great!"

"Ok. Then, it's settled. Andrea, I'll be back with your sleeping bag and pajamas."

"Thanks, Mom!" Andrea said as she gave her mom a big hug. As Mrs. Antenelli hugged her daughter, she caressed the top of her head, tucking a loose strand of hair behind her ear. I felt a sharp pang of something at this simple, loving gesture. I wasn't sure what it was but it left me feeling uneasy.

Andrea's mom returned soon with the sleeping bag and a few other items for Andrea.

"You two can stay up for another hour but I want you both in bed, teeth brushed, prayers said by 9 o'clock. Understood?"

"Ok, Mom."

"Yes, ma'am."

"Imari, you're so polite. Such good manners. Andrea, you could learn a thing or two from your friend here."

Andrea rolled her eyes and then placed her hand on her mom's back and led her out of the room. "Ok, Mom. Bye!"

Laughing, Mrs. Antenelli took the hint and left. "Have a good night, you two."

"Good night," we both said in unison.

We laid out our sleeping bags on the floor. Then Andrea disappeared to change into her pajamas and brush her teeth. I followed her to do the same. I pulled the small lamp next to my bed down to the floor and turned off the lights. We spent the next few hours laughing and talking about everything and nothing well past 9:00 p.m. Around 11:30 p.m., as we were both rallying back and forth with our yawns, Andrea said, "Do you ever wonder what happens to you when you die?"

"I don't know. I never thought about it. My mom said that, if you're good, you get to go to heaven and become an angel. And that you get to come back to earth and help the people you love. If that's true, then I know that's where my mom is."

"Yeah. You're right. She would be. Your mom is

the best. Do you think she can hear us now?"

I considered this for a moment. What if she could hear me, see me? Would she be disappointed in me? Did I cry too much? Not enough?

"I hope so," I finally said.

MARY

There are some days in your life that you'll remember forever. Yesterday was one of those days. What the Johnsons were going through—I just couldn't imagine. Imani had opened up to me a few weeks ago about her cancer and the baby. And when she lost the baby and needed to start chemo right away, it was me that she confided in and leaned on. I'll forever be grateful that I was able to be there for her during that time. But a couple of days ago, the worst had happened, and I can't get the image out of my head.

Imani and I had gotten into a routine. We'd shuffle the kids off to school and I'd drive down the hill and have coffee with Imani and try to get her to eat something before chemo.

"I'm just going to throw it up later," she'd always say.

Those weeks were priceless to me, and I could tell she needed me to know some things about her son, Imari—about their traditions and things Imari loved. She'd also made me swear never to tell him about the baby she'd lost. She'd named her Destiny. There was some irony in that name. I had thought it would make things harder for Imani to name the baby she'd lost but I didn't say this to her. I'd never lost a baby so why should I offer my opinion?

Then, during one of these trips to chemo, she'd asked me to raise Imari after she was gone. I was so overwhelmed by this. How hard it must be to have to ask another mother to raise your child—gut wrenching, powerless, hopeless. I was so overtaken with emotions that I had not even considered the logistics of it—legally. But she'd said that I would be doing both her husband and her son a great service and that Andrew and I would not likely face any resistance from either of them, father or son. This felt right when she said it. I had not seen George interact much with Imari but the little I did see was not good. He treated the child like a great disappointment. Imari would cling to his mom when his father entered the room, willing her to be a barrier between the two of them. When Imari would visit our house, it was clear that he was craving male attention. He was always so appreciative when Andrew would spend time with him and would ask so many questions. I could tell Andrew was happy about this too. He'd been patiently waiting for Jeffrey to get older so that he could impart his wisdom, but he was years away from that.

After that chemo session, I'd gone home and told

Andrew. He didn't hesitate in saying yes. I knew he would respond this way, but when he did, it was a relief. I had my talking points lined up ready for an argument just in case but it wasn't needed. Andrew didn't want to show it, but he was excited to be able to call Imari son—if it came to that. He'd been calling him son anyway since the day they'd met. Andrew then realized the gravity of this situation and what it would mean for all this to come to pass. Imari would have to lose his mother—the person he loved most in this world.

While that day was memorable, it wasn't the day I meant when I said there are days you never forget. The next day, after the kids were sent off to school, I made my way down to Imani's to have breakfast. I made my way up the front stairs of the house to knock on the door but there was no answer. My stomach dropped right away. For weeks now, I'd had this fear that something would happen—that I'd find Imani collapsed and would have to call an ambulance or worse. She'd given me a key but when I went to put the key in, I tried the knob first. The door was already unlocked. Makes sense. She'd just sent Imari off to school. I knocked again as I tried to open the door. It was stuck. I pushed a little harder this time and the door budged just a little, enough to understand what was happening. I put my back to the door and used my legs to drive the door open slowly and stepped through the doorway. On the floor, propped up against the back of the door, was Imani.

I'd fallen to her side, yelled her name, and slapped her face lightly to see if she'd respond. She wasn't breathing. I ran to the kitchen to the phone and called for an ambulance. They wanted to keep me on the phone but once I was sure they were on the way, I made my way back. I knelt beside her and held her hand. She had such a peaceful look on her face. She could have been dreaming.

It took forever for the ambulance to get there. I'd tried to reach George at work, but I was told that he was busy and couldn't get to the phone. I'd called Andrew and he said he would take care of getting in touch with George. When the ambulance arrived, the EMTs tried to get a pulse and had started to do chest compressions when they put her in the ambulance. I'd followed them to the ER in my car. I was too shocked to think when I was following the ambulance—going through red lights and weaving through traffic—my stomach still on the floor unlikely to leave that place until I knew for sure if she was gone.

But she was gone. Andrew had gone to the plant where George worked and had convinced the foreman that George needed to leave the assembly line and come with him to the hospital. Andrew had offered to drive him, but he'd told him no—that he was perfectly able to drive himself and that Andrew didn't need to bother coming to the hospital. Andrew had ignored him and followed anyway. He knew I was there and understood that I would need him.

George had gone right back and was back there for what felt like hours. Andrew held my hand tightly as we braced ourselves for the news. We couldn't do anything else. It almost felt like we were on the part of a rollercoaster that is diving towards the ground, waiting for the relief that comes when it levels off. But that relief was taking forever. After a couple of hours, George came out from behind the double doors of the ER and started toward the door. His eyes were blood red. He saw us and had intended to just continue walking past us when Andrew called after him.

"George, please wait."

"What? She's dead. I have to go," George said as tears started to form in his eyes and he violently wiped them away.

"She's, she's...no," I said. Andrew wrapped me in his arms and sat me down and let me weep for my friend. After fifteen minutes or so passed, Andrew looked at me. He'd been crying too.

"Sweetheart, I know that you're devasted. I am too. But we have to put that aside for now. We have to be there for Imari—our son."

Our son. Andrew had said that to me on purpose. He wasn't really our son. Not yet. But Andrew knew what I needed to hear in that moment. It had sobered me up and flipped a switch in me. Imani had asked us to care for her son, and that's what we were going to do. He needed us.

IMARI

In the morning, we were both awakened by Andrea's mom at the door. "Wake up, sleepy heads. Hmmm. Did you all stay up past bedtime?"

How could she tell? Moms always seemed to just know these things.

"Imari, why don't you go and take a shower and I'll pull out something for you to wear. Andrea, you're next. I'll bring you your clothes. Go on now," she said to both of us.

On my way out of the room, I asked Mrs. Antenelli, "Where's my dad?"

She seemed to measure her words. "Umm, he's at work, sweetheart."

"At work?" I was shocked by this. How could he just go to work like it was a normal day?

"Dear, he did try to get off of work but they wouldn't let him. He said they would fire him if he didn't come in. I can't believe it really. How could they be so insensitive? Trust me, honey, he does not want to be at work today."

I suddenly felt guilty that I had been so judgmental. I wondered if my mom could read my thoughts. I hoped that she couldn't.

Showered and dressed, we met Andrea's mom in the living room. She was there giving Jeffrey a bottle. As we entered the room, Jeffrey locked eyes with me so intensely, I had to look away. When I looked back, he was still staring at me.

"I think you have a new friend, Imari."

I smiled uncomfortably at this. Jeffrey squirmed in his mother's arms to get a better look at me.

"Here, Andrea, take your brother while I take some stuff out to the van."

"Come here, JJ," Andrea said as she reached out and took her brother from her mom and took a seat on the empty loveseat positioned in front of a large, street-facing window. Slowly, I sat next to Andrea. I'd obviously been around babies before—mainly in passing when I was with my mom at the grocery store or at church. This felt much different. I was suddenly very terrified that Andrea was going to ask me to hold him.

"JJ, this is Imari," Andrea said, taking his little

hand and waving it at me. Jeffrey's coloring was much different than Andrea's. While Andrea was fair like her mother, Jeffery had jet-black hair and very blue eyes. The contrast was striking. Now, those very blue eyes were locked on me. I didn't really know how to act around him.

Nervously, I smiled and said, "Hi, Jeffrey."

At this he let out a squeal-like laugh that made me laugh. Before I knew what was happening, Jeffrey was in my arms, exploring my face with his hands.

"Be careful, Imari. He's going to pull on your hair," Andrea said. At that exact moment, Jeffrey reached out to touch my hair but seemed surprised.

"I don't think he's ever touched hair like yours, Imari."

"Weird, huh, Jeffrey," I said as he bounced up and down in my arms at the sound of my voice.

"Wow. He really likes you!" Mrs. Antenelli said as she came back in the room. "Let me know if he starts to be too much for you."

"Yes, ma'am."

"Come on. Let me take you both to breakfast."

Andrea and I played card games in the house that day at her house. Jeffrey refused to leave my side and I didn't mind it at all. I wondered if he could feel the black hole of despair so alive in me, threatening to overtake me with every breath. But Jeffrey's laugh and pure joy brought me back from the depths. I envied him. The world for him was still filled with so much promise—new things to discover each day. He didn't yet know the sting of embarrassment or the soul-crushing loss of a parent. I started to realize that I was never going to truly feel joy again. It would always be tempered by the knowledge that anything I loved could be taken away. While it was true that my life had its challenges before my mom died, at least I had her to come home to. Now, there was no safe haven. The Antenellis were being very nice to me but I felt like I was trespassing—invading their beautiful, love-filled house with my dark cloud of grief. I could feel the tears coming.

"I think I wanna take a nap."

Andrea looked up from her cards full of concern but merely said, "You can sleep in my room."

Andrea got up and led me to her room. She pulled the curtains closed and handed me a large pink blanket. Her room was an explosion of pink—sickly sweet like cotton candy. I crawled on to her bed and under her pink blanket and I suddenly missed my own bed and protective blanket and grief pillow. When Andrea tried to leave with Jeffrey, he started to cry.

"JJ, Imari needs to take a nap. Sorry, Imari. I'll wake you up when it's time for dinner, ok?"

"Ok," I said from beneath the blanket.

I was asleep immediately. In my dream, my mom

was busying herself about the house.

"Imari, baby, grab the cooler from the garage for me."

"Yes, ma'am. Where are we going?"

"Oh, baby. You can't come with me on this adventure."

"But we always go on adventures together."

"Not this time, baby."

"That's not fair, Mom. Why can't I come with you? Mom? Mom?"

When I woke, I realized I was crying. Jeffrey was asleep in his crib next to me and Andrea was at her desk seated in her chair, looking at me.

"Bad dream about your mom?"

"Yeah."

"I heard you call out for her." I was suddenly slightly embarrassed. It still wasn't as bad as peeing yourself at a sleepover but if anyone else had heard me calling out for my mom in my sleep, it would only serve to further cement my nickname.

"Dinner's almost ready, if you want to wash your hands."

"Ok."

"Bathroom is right across the hall."

When I had finished washing up, Andrea took me to their den—a sunken room with orange-red shag carpeting and wood paneling. There, her father was smoking a cigar and reading his paper in his lounger.

When we entered the room, Mr. Antenelli put down his cigar and paper and closed the distance between us.

"Hi, Imari. It's good to see you again. We're all very sorry about your mom. We're here for you, son. Whatever you need."

"Thank you, sir."

"Sir. Do you hear that, Andrea? Sir."

At this, Andrea rolled her eyes and took my hand and led me to the dining room.

"We only really eat here on special occasions—like Thanksgiving, Christmas, or Easter. Mostly we eat at the kitchen table.

"Imari, honey. Do you want milk or water or soda?"

"Soda please."

"Soda? You never let me drink soda," Andrea said, crossing her arms in disgust.

"Fine. You can have soda too."

As we ate, I watched the Antenelli family. The feeling in the room felt much different than in my own. Here, every family member seemed to take up an equal amount of space with Jeffrey slightly edging everyone out. Mr. Antenelli didn't spend the time complaining about people in the world or his job. He asked his wife about her day and spoke to Jeffrey and asked me and Andrea how we'd spent the day. You could tell these people really loved being in each other's company. It was then that I started to think about my own future. What would dinner even be like with my mom gone? Would my dad expect me to cook and clean? Is that why Mom had spent so much time over the summer teaching me those things?

Friday was spent in much the same way but I knew that I was going back home when my father got home from work after dinner with the Antenellis.

"My dad is going to make pasta tonight. Homemade pasta, not out of the box. His grandmother taught him how to make it. She was from Italy. Do you know where Italy is?"

"Not really," I said.

"Anyway, it's really good. With meat sauce and garlic bread. We usually only eat it on Sundays when my dad doesn't have to work."

Seemed they were sending me off in style.

As we were around the table, there was suddenly a huge amount of dread. I didn't want to go back to a home where my mother wasn't there to brighten it. Mrs. Antenelli seemed to notice my change in mood.

"Imari, dear. It's been a pleasure having you stay here with us. You are always welcome here and at our dinner table. Ok? Truly. We all feel the same way." At this Jeffrey squealed, which everyone took to mean that he agreed as we all laughed.

"Thank you, Mrs. Antenelli, and you too Mr. Antenelli. This pasta is so good. And thank you too, Andrea."

Again, Jeffrey squealed and we all laughed.

"And you too, Jeffrey," I said still laughing.

When dinner was finished, I packed up my things and said my goodbyes.

"I'll walk down with you," Andrea said.

"Ok. Thanks for everything, Mr. and Mrs. Antenelli."

"You're welcome, Imari. Let us know if you need anything at all, ok?"

"Yes, ma'am."

As we walked down the hill towards my house, my feet began to feel like they were slogging through mud. I had not seen my father in days and, truthfully, I wasn't really looking forward to being alone in the house with him. Andrea was unusually quiet as we walked. I wondered what she was thinking. At the foot of my driveway, Andrea gave me a hug.

"If I don't see you tomorrow, I'll see you Sunday at the service," Andrea said.

"Ok. See ya later."

"Ok. Bye," Andrea said, waving at me as I turned and walked up the driveway.

As I opened the front door to the house, I felt a wave of sadness envelop me, weaving its way through all the hidden places in my soul. *This is the way I'm going to feel for the rest of my life*, I thought. Between the setting sun and all the drawn curtains, the house seemed to be in mourning as well. I tried to be as quiet as possible as I rounded the corner to my room but there, waiting for me at the end of the hall, was my father—drink in hand and smoking a cigarette. I was immediately enraged at the sight of this. Mom would have never let him smoke in the house.

"We're going to have to go get you a suit tomorrow."

Instead of responding, I just walked into my room, closed the door, undressed, and got under the covers of my bed—my grief pillow there to absorb the weight of my pain.

"Boy. I'm not gonna have you moping around this house forever. She's dead. The sooner you get over it and move on, the better."

I wrapped my pillow over my head, drowning out the drunken proclamations of my father as he continued on for minutes.

I was dreaming again. My mother was in the Voyageur. I'm trying to get to her, but I can't move my feet. I'm yelling but my voice isn't loud enough.

"Mom, wait! Take me with you!"

She doesn't hear me. She opens the window behind her head and looks back to find another version of herself.

"Where to, my queen?" she says to herself.

"Away from here," she answers.

13

IMARI

My dad and I had spent Saturday buying suits for each of us. He had no patience for this activity and barked his orders at me between swigs from the flask he kept in his pocket. I didn't mind speeding through this activity. I didn't want to be seen with him out in public by anyone from school. I wanted to be back home, in my bed. He had made me dress in my church clothes before we left the house but did not say why and I didn't ask. Once we had purchased the suits, we were on the road again but not headed home. I really didn't want to speak to him, but the question escaped from me before I could consider the consequence.

"Where are we going?"

"The wake."

"What's a wake?"

At this, my father was incensed. He took his right hand off the wheel and hit me across the side of the head, knocking my head against the window. I was stunned. My father had never hit me before this. He never really seemed to care enough to be bothered with disciplining me. I decided in that moment not to say another word to him again for as long as I could.

As we pulled up to the funeral home, I surveyed the cars in the parking lot. How many people were going to be in here? Would it just be family members or would people from school be here as well? My father refilled his flask with a bottle of whiskey from the glove compartment.

"Get out, boy. I don't want you acting like a baby when you get in there. Don't embarrass me."

I got out of the car quickly and started walking towards the entrance a few steps behind my father. As we walked up the stairs to the funeral home, a large, balding black man greeted us with a somber smile.

"Mr. Johnson. I'm Alfred Montgomery. We spoke on the phone. We are so sorry for your loss. Please come inside. You have quite a few people here already waiting to pay their respects. Please follow me."

As we walked inside, I was immediately hit with a strange aroma. It was a musty smell fighting with the smell of flowers.

I could hear the murmuring of voices in the room ahead that had two French-curtained doors closed, muffling the sound. As Mr. Montgomery opened the door, I was flooded with conversations and with faces that I recognized—mostly family. I wasn't really used to seeing my family. I always thought it was odd that they never visited but I never thought to ask my mother why.

"Mr. Johnson, when you're ready, we'll lead your guests through those other set of doors there to pay their respects. Before we do, would you like some time alone with your wife for you and your son?"

"No, Alfred. Thanks. You can open the doors now."

"Yes, sir. Of course."

I was both confused and relieved. Was my mother's body in that room? Why? I had never been to something like this before. While I was alive when my grandparents passed, I was too young to remember them or their passing. Would she just be laying there on a table or in a bed? I was suddenly very glad that my dad didn't send me in there alone.

As people started to pour through the doors, I slowly moved away from my father towards the back of the crowd when I suddenly bumped into someone.

"Oh, sorry," I said, turning around to see the warm face of my English teacher, Mrs. Hunt.

"Hi, Imari dear. How are you doing?"

"Ok."

"This here is my son Jacob. Jacob, come here and say hello. This is Imari."

A tall, freckled boy approached. He looked like he didn't feel altogether comfortable in his body, like one day he'd woken up with his limbs several inches longer and had been trying to adjust to the change ever since.

"Hello," Jacob said in a much deeper voice than I had expected out of his wiry frame.

"Hello."

"Imari, do you want us to walk in with you? Here, take my hand."

I was suddenly overwhelmed by this kindness and started to weep. I collapsed into Mrs. Hunt's side when I felt a hard grip on my arm, yanking me away from the warmth of my teacher.

"I told you not to embarrass me, boy. Now get in there and say goodbye to your dead mother."

Mrs. Hunt interjected, "Mr. Johnson. I'm so sorry for your loss. I was just telling Imari that we'd be happy to walk in with him."

"No. He needs to do this on his own. I'm not raising a weak boy who can't face hard things in life."

Mrs. Hunt simply nodded her head and then approached me and took my hand. "Imari, I'm here if you need me. I'm not sure when you're back to school but we've been working on our first poems in class. Maybe you can write yours and have it ready when you return? It should be about a time that brought you great joy and happiness. Think you could do that?"

"Yes ma'am. Thank you."

My father then grabbed me by the shoulder and pushed me through the doors. I could feel the eyes of the people in the room on me. This was all happening so fast.

"Go!" my father said as he gave me a push forward, causing me to stumble.

I moved forward slowly with my eyes on the old carpet—red with gold diamond-shaped ornate squares. This carpet was in need of a good cleaning. How many grieving families had made this walk along this carpet to forever have the image of their loved ones changed? Would this now be the image of my mother who would show up in my dreams?

As I approached the casket, I could see that it was open and that there was someone in it. I didn't have the courage yet to look at this person's face. Their hands were clasped, one over the other. Those hands. I recognized those hands. They were the hands of the person who made my breakfast, who took me on adventures, who caressed my face when I was sad. Now standing at the casket, I could hear a swell of sniffles behind me. For a moment, I considered turning around and walking back but when I looked over my shoulder, I saw the stern, disapproving face of my father. So, as I turned back around, I saw her. She never wore this much makeup but she did look like herself. She almost could have been sleeping. I reached out and touched her hand but it no longer held the warmth that I knew to be my mother. She was gone and my life was never going to be the same again.

14

IMARI

Sunday had started like any other day. Those moments as you're just waking up, anything is possible. But then, as you wake, you are hit with your new reality and suddenly it's clear that the only thing on your agenda for the day is an intense emptiness that leaves you with no hope. And you realize that you will never feel joy again.

Throughout the day, from the funeral to the gathering after, I pulled deeper into myself. I was at my father's side all day so I didn't feel like I could cry— even if I had wanted to. Instead, I was left mute, unable to summon the force required to initiate my voice. As they put my mother in the ground, I focused my attention on my own hands. I had never really noticed it before this moment but they were my mother's hands. For a very brief moment, I had the smallest light—a sense of connection to my mother. But just like that, it was gone again. These were my hands—not my mother's. Nothing great had been created by these hands. They didn't bring warmth or comfort to anyone. All I wanted in that moment was to disappear.

Back home after the long day, I retreated to my room but very soon after, I was met by a knock on the door.

"Boy, you're going back to school tomorrow. I need to work so you need to go to school. So, get your clothes out. You're going to have to set your own alarm, make your own breakfast, and ride the bus. And here's a key to the house. Don't lose it or you'll just have to sit outside until I get home."

I reached over and set the alarm next to my bed and went to the bathroom to brush my teeth. Back in bed, I squeezed my pillow and quickly fell asleep.

I saw my mother. She was in the Voyageur. I was pleading with her not to leave. I chased behind her as she pulled out of the driveway, out of the neighborhood, and on to the main road. I was continuing to chase her—desperate not to lose her. Then, I realized where we were. We were back at the funeral home. In the distance, I saw my mother get out of the truck and slowly walk towards the entrance. She was wearing a white, flowing sundress that looked striking against her deep chocolate skin. I was still several yards away and running as fast as I could, but I was running through mud—deep and restrictive. I was clawing through it with my hands and kicking hard with my legs. When I finally arrived at the entrance and opened the door, I saw my mother standing at the front of the room beyond the double doors in front of an empty casket. When I entered, she looked back at me and smiled, opened the casket, and lowered herself into it.

I was screaming now.

"Mom! Mom, no! Please! Don't go!"

My feet wouldn't move as the casket rolled away on its own into the back of a hearse.

When I woke, I realized that I was crying and that I must have been screaming as my voice was hoarse. I glanced over at my digital clock. It was 3:33 a.m. I rolled over, the scenes from my nightmare still etched in my brain. I desperately did not want to fall back asleep.

When I woke again, it was because I heard the bus driving by my house. I shot up and started to throw on some clothes I had lying on the floor. There was no time for breakfast or for brushing my teeth. I'd have one more chance to catch the bus as the bus made a loop and would stop again on the corner. I grabbed the house key and my bookbag and ran out the door, locking it behind me.

I got to the bus, zipping up my pants just as the bus pulled up. How embarrassing would that have been? When I got on the bus, Andrea was seated next to Angie. There was a seat open across from them and Andrea waved me over as she convinced the girl seated there to move over towards the window to allow me to sit on the aisle.

"Hi Imari," Angie said. "I'm so sorry about your mom."

"Thank you."

"I didn't know you were coming to school today, Imari. I would have come down the road and stood at the bus stop with you," Andrea said.

"That's ok. My dad said I had to go back today because he had to work."

"Oh, ok." I could tell Andrea wanted to say more but was biting her tongue.

"Hey, look! E-mommy made it back to school. Guess we'll have to come up with a new name for you though, huh? Maybe...E-dead-Mommy," Bruce said, as LeDarius and others laughed a bit uncomfortably.

It felt like a punch in the gut. I'm not sure what I was expecting. Maybe I thought I'd have a little reprieve from my tormentors—at least for a few weeks. I was already in tears, and they were coming furiously—a broken dam of emotions.

"You're an ass, Bruce," Andrea said. "How would

you feel if your mom had just died and we were making fun of her? I guess we'll get a chance to find out if she keeps smoking crack."

At this, Bruce lunged at her, and I jumped up to throw myself in his path. As I did, Bruce collided into me hard, knocking me backwards, my head ramming into the hard metal edge of the seat.

Over the intercom, the bus driver demanded we get back into our seats. He hadn't seen what happened. Andrea was standing over me, pulling me to my feet, but I felt uneasy. I reached back to touch the back of my head and felt the sting of broken skin. When I looked at my hand, it was stained with blood.

"Haha! I cracked E-dead Mommy's head open. That's what you get for getting in the way. Next time, you should just let me smack the shit out of your little loud-mouthed girlfriend."

"Ignore him, Imari. Are you ok? Here," Andrea said as she reached inside her pink leather purse and pulled out a pink bandana. "It's clean. Use it to stop the bleeding. You should go see the nurse as soon as we get to school in case you need to go get stitches."

My head was throbbing with pain. All I wanted was to be back home in my bed, squeezing my pillow.

Off the bus, I quickly made my way to the nurse. Andrea was in tow behind me.

"God, he's such a jerk. I hate him. I wish he would just die." Andrea caught herself—concerned that she might offend me by saying the word die. She quickly tried to move past it. "I'll walk with you to the nurse and then I'll go let Mr. Smith know where you are."

I nodded.

"Hi, Nurse Rangles," Andrea said to the school nurse who was neatly dressed in her all-white uniform sipping her morning coffee.

"Oh, dear. Did someone slip and fall this morning?"

"No—"

"Yes. I fell getting off the bus," I said as I stole a quick look at Andrea and shook my head. Nurse Rangles seemed to notice this but decided not to press it.

"Andrea, sweetheart. Run along and let Mr. Smith know that Imari is here with me, ok?"

"Yes ma'am," Andrea said.

Ma'am. I'd never heard her say that before. I must be rubbing off on her. I smiled slightly at the thought of that but was immediately brought back to the present with my searing head pain.

Once Andrea was gone, Nurse Rangles looked at me warmly. "Now, do you want to tell me what actually happened?"

I considered this for a moment and decided it was better to stick with the lie. Looking down at my feet, I said, "I slipped and fell and hit my head."

"Ok. Well, let's see what we're dealing with."

She reached back and took my hand away from my wound. The pink bandana was covered in my blood.

She saturated a large ball of cotton in some brown liquid and started to clean the blood on my head.

"The good news is that the bleeding has stopped, mostly. You did a good job keeping pressure on the wound. But we should probably get you to see a doctor in case you need stitches. We'll need to call your father—"

"No! Please, don't call him. He won't come anyway. Can you just take me, Nurse Rangles?"

Sympathetically, she looked down at me and caressed the side of my face. I was immediately reminded of my mother, and I reached up to touch her hand as I leaned my face into her touch. Something wet was falling on both of our hands. She had that same warmth of my mother. A touch that made you feel like everything would be ok. When I realized the water was from my eyes and that I was crying again, I sat up quickly and wiped my eyes. Nurse Rangles quickly turned around and wiped her eyes as well.

"Wait here."

I waited with my feet hanging over the small hospital bed in Nurse Rangles' office. What a horrible way to come back to school, I thought. *It must be an omen of things to come. I should have just stayed home from school. My father wouldn't know if I did.*

After a few minutes, Nurse Rangles returned, looking a little flustered.

"Ok, Imari, dear. Grab your coat and bag and follow me."

In the parking lot, we walked up to an old green sedan with a green interior.

"Oh, just move those aside," Nurse Rangles said, looking slightly embarrassed. "I wasn't expecting anyone to see my car in this state."

I smiled up at her and climbed inside. I'm not sure what I was expecting her car to look like. Her office is so neat and sterile, but her car was the opposite. There were fast food wrappers in the back seat, a bag of curlers on the floor next to my feet, and I could have sworn I saw something move out the corner of my eye but I decided I must have been seeing things.

I had to get seven stitches, which wasn't that bad. The worst part was that they had to shave part of my hair off to get to it. So now I had a patch of hair missing and gauze wrapped around my head to make sure my dressing staying in place. I begged Nurse Rangles to just take me home. I said that I had a key and that my father would be fine with it but she insisted that I go back to school. By the time we made it back to school, it was time for Mrs. Hunt's English class. She had apparently been made aware of my situation ahead of time as she didn't seem surprised to see me wrapped in gauze.

"Imari, dear, please have a seat. We are reading our poems. Natalie, please continue with your poem."

"Ok."

And since I was a little girl
These memories would always bring
The joy of flying through the air
In the backyard on my swing

The room burst with applause.

"Great job, Natalie!" one girl said.

"That was amazing!" said another.

"Ok. Who's next? Any volunteers? No. Well, ok. I'll choose then. Bruce, why don't you go?"

LeDarius and Bruce both started laughing under their breath and Bruce walked to the front of the room.

Bruce cleared his throat and began

There once was a little boy
Who everyone thought was strange
And everywhere his mommy went
The boy would do the same

But now she's dead and in the ground
And the worms are having a meal
And the little wimpy boy just cries and cries
Like the noises from a seal

I hope—

"Enough. Bruce, have a seat. Hand me that paper."

Mrs. Hunt took a red marker and wrote a large "F" on the page big enough for the entire class to see.

"Bruce Jackson. The assignment was to write

about something that brings you joy."

"That's what I did."

I could feel everyone's eyes on me, but I refused to look up from my desk. I just wanted to disappear. At the end of the class, Mrs. Hunt asked me to hang back.

"How's your head, sweetheart?"

"Ok."

"I'm so sorry about that awful poem. I'll be sharing that with the principal. Let me know if you need anything, ok?"

"Yes, ma'am."

I could feel the tears coming so I made my way to the door of the classroom and out to catch up with the rest of my class at lunch.

As soon as I walked through the door, Bruce and LeDarius spotted me and began their mocking.

"He looks like a mummy! Haha. E-mummy!"

"Do you think that's what your dead mommy looks like? Hey, little punk. Answer me when I talk to you."

I turned quickly and headed for the lunch line but I didn't get out of reach fast enough. Bruce tripped me from behind and I went stumbling forward, falling face first on to the ground, my forehead taking the brunt of the fall.

I was overcome with an all-consuming sense of hopelessness that far exceeded any sort of embarrassment. I just stayed on the ground in tears. I was soon being scooped up by the familiar warmth of Mrs. Hunt.

"What happened here?" Mrs. Hunt yelled so loudly that you could suddenly hear a pin drop. "Is there no one who is willing to tell the truth?"

Everyone knew the rules of engagement here. You rat, you become the next target and as sympathetic as many likely were to my plight, there weren't any who were willing to take my place.

"Imari, sweetheart, are you ok?"

A huge knot had started to form on my head. I was too distraught to respond. I pulled myself up and walked to the lunch line, though there really was no point. I had no desire to eat. Mrs. Hunt returned to the teacher's table and became engrossed in conversation, which is why she missed what happened next. I didn't really notice it right away myself, but I was suddenly covered in milk and I saw Bruce and LeDarius off in the distance laughing. They had convinced someone else to do their dirty work for them. The milk soaked through my bandage.

I had had enough. I got up from the table and walked down the main hall of the school and out the front door and on to the main road. I had forgotten my jacket back at school and the crisp fall air hit my milk-covered head sharply but I didn't care. I didn't care if I froze to death or was hit by a car or was lost, never to be seen again. In fact, it's exactly what I wanted. Maybe then, I could see my mother again.

Moments later, I heard a horn honking in the distance. I refused to turn around. Hopefully, it was some oncoming traffic accident that would wrap itself around me and carry me off into the beyond. But the horn continued as the car got closer. Then I heard the crunching of gravel as the car pulled off onto the shoulder of the road behind me.

"You stop right there, Mister," Nurse Rangles said. I stopped and turned around. "Where exactly do you think you're going?"

"Home."

"Imari, get in the car."

Ever polite, I shuffled my feet towards Nurse Rangles' car and, for the second time that day, tried to ignore the mess around my feet.

Back at school, Nurse Rangles sat me down in a chair and inspected my newest injury.

"You're having a bad day, huh?"

That was an understatement, I thought, but decided not to respond.

"Here, put this bag of ice on your forehead and jump up here on the exam table. I need to make sure you don't have a concussion, again."

She began shining light into my eyes for the second time that day and assessed that I was fine and allowed me to lie down.

"No sleeping though. Just to be safe."

After several moments of the bag of ice on my head, Nurse Rangles returned with some juice and cookies. Suddenly I was ravenous and devoured them.

"Wow. You must have been hungry. Did you eat lunch?" I shook my head. "Ok. Well, here's a sandwich. It's egg salad. Do you like egg salad?"

It wasn't my favorite but I was far too hungry to say so.

I spent the afternoon assisting Nurse Rangles in her office—organizing files, cleaning counters. It seemed like she was going to let me stay here the rest of the school day but I didn't want to ask. When the occasional student would come in to see Nurse Rangles, she would send me to her attached office and have me close the door so the student would have some privacy though I could still hear. The most common issue seemed to be tummy aches that were resolved by a dose of the pink stuff. In between student visits, Nurse Rangles would give me a new task to do. When she finally ran out of tasks, she asked if I had any homework to do. I recalled that Mrs. Hunt had asked me to write a poem about the thing that brought me the most joy, so I started writing.

I was surprised at how quickly it came to me—like the words had been queued up waiting to be put to paper. In a half an hour, I was finished as tears stained the page. This was going to be impossible to read in front of the class. Suddenly, I thought I should just throw it away. Bruce and LeDarius would have a field day with this. Instead, I tucked it deep into my book bag.

When the final minutes of the day approached, I started to gather up my things for another ride in the green mess mobile. But to my dismay, Nurse Rangles asked, "Are you able to take the bus home, sweetheart? I need to pick my son up from school."

It never occurred to me that she might have her own children to take care of. My brief respite in Nurse Rangles' office was over and so was my slightly improved mood. The cloud of hopelessness that had engulfed me all day was back again. Now, my goal was to get to the bus stop as soon as possible and get a seat next to the bus driver. Surely I'd be safe there.

The bell rang and I thanked Nurse Rangles for everything and raced to the bus. The halls were flooded with other students in a hurry to get as far away from school as possible. I tried to walk fast enough to get to the bus quickly but not so fast as to draw undue attention to myself. Even so, I could still feel students' eyes on me as I passed—bandaged head, knot still prominent on my forehead.

At the bus, I quickly got on and grabbed a seat directly behind the bus driver. I felt a brief moment of relief as other students started to fill the bus. Andrea and Angie were one of the last few to get on the bus and took a seat near the back. Andrea had kept her distance from me since the events of the morning. I didn't blame her. No need to rush into the burning building if you're safe outside. I'm sure I'd do the same if I was in her shoes. A worm of an idea started to form. Something I had not considered before this moment. *I deserve what's happening to me. I am weird and different. There is something wrong with me so it's no wonder that I am a target. If only I was normal.* My soul seemed to latch on to this idea, weaving itself to it—wrapped and entangled. I was so caught up in this idea that I didn't notice that Bruce and LeDarius had taken a seat just two rows back from me and well within earshot.

"How much of her body do you think the worms have eaten?" Bruce asked—laughing. LeDarius laughed at this but didn't seem as committed to it as Bruce. "They've probably eaten her face off like in Indiana Jones."

I wanted desperately not to have this image start to form in my head but there it was, and I was weeping at the thought of it.

"Oh, look. Baby is crying again. What a little punk! You crying for your dead mommy?"

I could hear that the conversations around me had stopped, and they were all listening and watching me. Then I heard Bruce whispering to a kid behind me. He had to be in the first grade.

"Do it or you'll turn into a little punk like him!"

I felt bad for the kid. *Whatever he'd asked him to do, he should just do it,* I thought. Nothing was worth this torment. Then suddenly, a huge thud against the back of my head—a full can of soda dangerously close to where I had gotten stitches. The boy behind me had dissolved into tears. This had finally gotten the bus driver's attention.

"Y'all bet not be throwin' things on my bus!"

Bruce and LeDarius laughed at this.

Finally, they both got off the bus and the little boy behind me shyly asked if I was ok and apologized profusely—still in tears.

"It's ok. It's not your fault," I said to the weepy boy.

At my bus stop, I quickly descended the stairs and ran to my front door. I could hear Andrea calling to me from behind, but I was in no mood to engage with her today.

I opened the door to the house, and closed and locked it behind me. I ran to my room, took off my school clothes and climbed into bed, clutching my pillow. *There's something wrong with you. You deserve this. There's something wrong with you. You deserve this.*

Again, and again this refrain permeated my thoughts until another thought emerged.

I don't want to be here anymore. I wish I was dead.

GEORGE

If there was ever any goodness in me, it died today when I put my wife in the ground. She was the only one who could ever see that in me. I didn't deserve her. I only wish that I had let her know how much she meant to me while she was here. It's too late now. What I do deserve is to feel like this—my insides hallowed out and filled with liquor—sloshing around against the shell of my soul. My house was filled with people today, saying how much Imani meant to them and how sorry they were for me and the boy. I had no patience for it.

At the gravesite, those people who claimed to be her family tried to pay their respects but I was having none of that.

"What the fuck are you doing here?"

"She was my—"

"She wasn't anything to you. You disowned her, remember? You don't get to show up now that she's dead and pretend you cared about her. You discarded her like some piece of unwanted furniture. So, you don't get to call yourself her mother or say that she was your daughter. That was a decision you made. So fuck all the way off and take the rest of your disgusting family with you."

They wiped their fake tears and crawled into their car and drove away. I smiled a little at that scene.

I think Imani would have been proud of how I cast them out. Vengeance.

I had the boy at my side all day. I don't know why I resent this kid so much. Maybe I was jealous because of the relationship he had with my wife. He was able to do the very thing I could not—let his mother know how much he loved her every day. I tried to separate the two of them, but he'd always follow her around like some lovesick puppy—hanging on to her every word. It pissed me off really. So, it was a relief when I had gotten the letter from that attorney telling me of Imani's wishes. It would take a few weeks to make it through the paperwork. Until then, I was just going to try to avoid him. Hell, it was the best thing I could do for both of us.

15

IMARI

When I woke, I looked over at my clock. No way! It was 3:33 a.m. again. What were the odds of that? I had managed to avoid my father, which was great. I didn't want to have to deal with all his questions about my injuries and then have him tell me what a little sissy I was turning into.

I quickly set my alarm clock so that I wouldn't have to rush again this morning and went across the hall to the bathroom. I couldn't see the back of my head, but I knew I had a big chunk of hair missing where my stitches were. If only I had another mirror, I would be able to see it. I knew my mom had one in her purse that was still sitting on the counter in the kitchen. I decided I would go fetch it as I made myself a sandwich. I was so hungry.

In the kitchen, I fetched the mirror from my mom's purse. It felt strange to be going into her purse without her permission. But then, she wasn't here to give it to me. I made a sandwich from the spiral ham in the refrigerator. I attempted to cut the sandwich diagonally into triangles like my mom used to do but I didn't quite get the angle right. I wolfed down the sandwich quickly with a glass of milk. I washed my dishes, dried them, and put them back in the cabinet. I didn't want there to be any evidence that I was there. I then shuffled my way back to the bathroom, making sure to avoid the squeaky floorboards.

Back in the bathroom, I sat up on the counter in front of the large mirror and took my mom's mirror—angling it so that I could see the back of my head. I slowly removed the bandage and was met with some resistance. It was caught on the stitches. I was afraid to pull too hard for fear that I would rip the stitches out, so I gingerly pulled at the bandage until it was free. Nurse Rangles had sent me home with instructions on how to clean it and apply a new bandage. When I saw the wound, it suddenly started to hurt again. I reached back to touch it with my fingers and felt the prickly stitches.

Nurse Rangles mentioned that it was important that I let the wound get some air when I was awake but to cover it when I was asleep. I decided I could probably just sleep on my stomach since that's the position I usually slept in anyway and I'd change my alarm for a few minutes earlier to give myself more time to redress the wound in the morning. Still sleepy, I got back in the bed and was quickly back to sleep.

I was abruptly awakened by the screaming of my alarm clock. Desperate to turn it off, I reached through the air, fumbling at the clock searching for the off switch. There was a snooze button on here somewhere. I think my mom purposely didn't show it to me for fear I would overuse it. Remembering that I needed to deal with my wound, I jumped up and headed over to the bathroom. I had hidden my supplies under the sink behind a stack of magazines and cleaning products. Maybe I would be able to avoid my father long enough that he wouldn't even notice. The knot on my forehead was still there, though not as prominent. I discovered though that if I positioned the gauze just right, I could completely cover it.

I quickly dressed and had breakfast. The trip to school, though shorter than the ride home from school, seemed to be the worse of the two. Something about the morning gave Bruce extra energy for his destructive tendencies. I gathered my things and headed towards the bus stop when I noticed Andrea there. I had almost forgotten that she was going to be there since she was so silent yesterday.

"Hi Imari," she said, looking sheepishly down at the ground.

I nodded in response.

"I'm so sorry about everything that happened yesterday. I know I wasn't a good friend to you. It was all just so shocking. I've been at this school long enough now that I shouldn't be surprised really. But I was. I just didn't know kids could be this mean. And I'm ashamed to say, I was so afraid yesterday when Bruce lunged at me, so afraid that I just wanted to be as far away from him as possible which meant being far away from you. I talked to my parents about it, and they were so angry. They said they were going to come to the school today and talk to the principal. My dad said he was going to have a chat with your dad about—"

"No!"

"What?"

"Please. Please tell your dad not to talk to mine. He's just going to make things worse for me."

"Oh. I think he already did. Before your dad left for work this morning."

"Great." *Another fantastic start to the day*, I thought.

"I'm sorry, Imari. He thought he needed to know what was happening."

"He's just going to blame me for it."

Andrea considered this for a moment. Fortunately, the bus pulled up and we got on. Angie had saved a seat for Andrea and I took a seat toward the back of the bus. As soon as I sat down, I saw a letter slide under the seats just under my feet addressed, "Dear Imari." I reached down and picked it up. When I turned it over it read, "From Beyond the Grave." I knew I shouldn't open it. I heard Bruce and LeDarius laughing—though it was mainly Bruce. I opened the envelope and pulled out a sheet of paper. On it was a drawing but I immediately noticed the most disturbing part. They had cut out my mother's picture from her obituary and used it in the drawing. My mother in a coffin, worms everywhere. There was a bubble coming out from her mouth and it read, "Help, Imari. They're eating me!"

I balled the letter up and threw it on the ground.

As we arrived at school and were getting off the bus, Bruce sidled up behind me.

"You like my drawing, you little sissy?"

I was quickly trying to get off the bus, but Bruce pushed me into the person in front of me.

"Hey," the girl in front of me said.

"Sorry," I said.

"Yeah! Watch where you're going, sissy," Bruce said with venom in his voice.

I quickly maneuvered my way off the bus and headed straight to Nurse Rangles' office. She had asked me to stop by on my way to homeroom so that she could check my wound.

As I entered her office, she greeted me with a big smile and hug. It was moments before I realized that

I was still holding on to her.

"Oh, hey. Come here. Are you ok, sweetheart?"

Quickly I pulled myself together. "Yes ma'am."

Nurse Rangles looked concerned but didn't press.

"Ok. Let's see how you did dressing your wound. Did you give it time to breathe last night?"

"Yes ma'am."

"Your father is going to need to take you in to your family doctor to have those stitches removed in a few weeks. Two weeks, I think the doctor said. But your family doctor will know when to take them out. You're probably going to need to keep your hair shaved around the wound. Maybe you should just buzz the rest of your hair."

The thought of walking around the school with a buzzed head, knot on my forehead, stitches in the back, just screamed, "Make fun of me!"

Nurse Rangles checked the wound and praised my dressing and sent me off to homeroom with another hug.

"I hope you have a better day today. It can't get much worse than yesterday, right?" She smiled warmly down at me.

"Ok. Thanks, Nurse Rangles."

"You're welcome, sweetheart."

When I arrived to homeroom, the entire class turned to look at me as I entered. "Thanks for joining us finally, Imari," Mr. Smith said.

"I was with the nurse."

At this, he seemed to notice my head dressing for the first time. "Very well. Please have a seat."

As I went to sit down, there was a sheet of paper in my seat. It was the same drawing as on the bus. When I crumbled it up, Bruce turned around and said, "I have a lot more where that came from, punk. And I've put them all over the school." He laughed maniacally.

"Bruce and Imari, what's so funny back there? Would you like to share your joke with the class?"

Neither of us responded. I felt a sickness rumbling at the pit of my stomach. How many copies had he made of this drawing? I didn't want the entire school seeing my mother in this way. My mouth started to water. It was coming. I jumped up from my seat.

"Imari, sit down!" Mr. Smith yelled loudly at me. But I was out the door, rushing to the boys' room. I burst inside and just made it to the stall when I threw up—an exorcism of my morning breakfast.

Slowly I got up from the bathroom floor and made my way to the sink and washed out my mouth with water. I looked up and caught a glimpse of myself. I didn't recognize what I saw in my eyes. There was an emptiness—devoid of any light. I wiped my mouth with a paper towel and shuffled back to homeroom.

"Look who has decided to rejoin us. The next time you jump up and run out of my classroom, young man, that'll mean detention."

"But he was sick," Andrea said.

"Did I ask you for your commentary, Ms. Antenelli? Maybe both of you would like detention?"

At this, Andrea hung her head and turned back around in her seat.

The rest of the morning proceeded without much incident. It was on my way to English class that I saw them strewn all about the floor—that disgusting picture of my mom. I reached down, grabbing as many of them as I could but I was too late. Other students had picked them up too and were now looking at me with forlorn faces.

Mrs. Hunt greeted us warmly at the door to her classroom.

"Good morning, my lovely fifth graders! Why all the glum faces?" At this, one of the students handed her the drawing and she audibly gasped.

"Who did this?" she said, almost whispering to the female student who handed her the drawing. That student whispered something back to her as Mrs. Hunt leaned in to hear. Mrs. Hunt stood back up and demanded we all go into her classroom and have a seat.

"Except for you two," she said, pointing at Bruce and LeDarius.

"What? I ain't do nothin'!" Bruce said.

"Me neither," argued LeDarius.

"Come. Now. We'll see what the principal has to say about this."

Now I had never really been to see Principal Chambers, but I'd heard horror stories. Children leaving in tears. Parents yelling. Toys forever locked up in his glass cabinet—a reminder to all office visitors of the punishment for bringing a toy to school except for show-and-tell days. Of course, this fate was too good for Bruce and LeDarius. They shouldn't be going to see the principal. They should be going to see a warden in some maximum-security prison.

When Mrs. Hunt returned, she still seemed shaken at what she had seen. She sat down on her stool at the front of the class and addressed the class.

"I'm always surprised by the cruelty of some children. Each year, it seems to get worse and the students younger. But this. I have never seen such a display of such utter disregard for the suffering of others. All year, I have been trying to teach you all about the power words have. How they can unlock new universes and fill you with such joy. But you have all now learned another lesson about the power of words. They can also be used to cause great pain. And when we see this, it is our responsibility—we, the carriers of light and joy, to stand up and fight against that evil. Even the smallest light can dispel the darkest of darkness."

The class hung tightly to every word Mrs. Hunt said. There were moments in your life that you always remember—those that leave an indelible mark. I had the sense that this was that moment for a lot of us in that room.

"Now class, I need someone to bring some joy back to this room. We only have a few students left who haven't read us their poems." Searching her list, she zeroed in on a name. "Imari, dear. Have you had a chance to complete the assignment? It's perfectly understandable if you haven't."

My palms were suddenly moist with sweat, throat dry. Then I realized, with Bruce and LeDarius gone, this was probably the best time to read my poem.

"Yes, ma'am. I finished it."

"Oh, great! Please students, let's give Imari a round of applause as he comes forward to read his poem."

The class seemed to be waiting for the opportunity to give us this expression of support and erupted in applause. It was so loud, it almost had the opposite effect of making me want to stay in my seat. But I summoned the courage to get out of my chair and go to the front of the class, notebook in hand. Mrs. Hunt moved her stool to the side but was closer to me than she had been when others read their poems. She gave me an encouraging nod and I began.

The Scent of the Lilies

I know the task that was given
Was to describe what brings us joy

And I'll do that by describing the love
Between a mother and her boy.

She was light itself and no one else
Had the power she could bring
To illuminate the darkest places
Bring a gleam to everything.

She would craft stories of princes
Damsels in distress
And quests with great allure,
Quests with her at the lead
And me at the back of our trusty Voyageur.

There are so many moments when I look back
That bring such joy to me
But most of them are the simple moments
Within my family.

Small chats at the breakfast table
A caress of my face
The warmth of the touch of her hand
The way she always would sit and listen
Seeking always to understand.

But perhaps most of all
Are the memories we had
Next to the pond at the end of the trail
Where we would feed the ducks

And give them names like, Johnny, Luke, or Dale.

And around that pond were flowers
Whose smell will bring joy to me
Every time I smell those flowers, I'll smile
At the scent of the lilies.

When I looked up, Mrs. Hunt was wiping tears from her eyes and several of the other students were too—mostly the girls but a few of the boys too. Then, Mrs. Hunt stood from her seat and started clapping and the other students followed suit. If I could have turned red, I would have. I'm sure I was, under my brown skin. The applause seemed to go on forever. I could only stand there a couple of seconds before I hurried back to the safety of my desk. But the applause followed me and before I knew it, I was overwhelmed with tears. I was immediately swarmed by some students hugging me and some still clapping. The cloud of despair that I had wrapped myself in the past few days started to melt away. I felt the love being poured into me by my fellow students, my friends.

16

IMARI

The warm connected feeling I felt in English class carried over into lunch—a place recently fraught with embarrassment and a desire to disappear. I looked around to see if Bruce or LeDarius had rejoined us, but they were nowhere to be found. News spread throughout the lunchroom of the picture and how Bruce and LeDarius were sent to the principal's office. There was also another piece of gossip starting to bubble its way through the crowd—a complicated game of telephone as the news made its way to the table where I was sitting with Andrea, Angie, and a few other students from my English class who were also still feeling the love and connection.

"They've both been suspended!" one girl said.

"What?" Andrea said.

"Bruce and LeDarius. They've been suspended," another girl said. "My friend, Jessica, who is in Mrs. Shropshire's class, said they saw Bruce's dad carrying him out of school by his arm—yelling at him. Saying what an F-up he was. 'Just like your idiot brother,' he said."

"Good," Andrea said. "They should have been expelled for what they did."

Later that day, we'd find out that Andrea's father, as promised, happened to already be at the school raising the issue of what had happened on the bus and in the cafeteria the previous day when Mrs. Hunt showed up with the two students. Their fates were sealed.

I floated through the rest of the day. It was unknown how long Bruce and LeDarius would be suspended but the mere thought of not having to ride the bus with either of them for a few days felt like a dream. To not have the acid rise in my stomach at the sound of the final bell of the day. To be able to get on the bus and sit anywhere with no fear of being hit in the head, or tripped, or made fun of—it was unbelievable. I laughed with Andrea and Angie and a few other students on the bus.

The weather was starting to get a little cooler but that day, it was beautiful. The sun shone through the windows of the bus, creating incredible shadows on the floor. I felt so light. I wanted to feel this way all the time.

When we arrived at our bus stop, Andrea and I got off the bus, laughing at some joke someone had made at Bruce' expense. The bus pulled away and Andrea and I were still laughing. At the end of my driveway, Andrea gave me a hug.

"This was the weirdest day. It started so terribly, but the end was amazing. I hope it continues to get better for you and me both," Andrea said as she turned and started to walk home.

"Me too."

As I stood there and watched Andrea walk up the street, I smiled—a smile from deep within. I was nearly to my door before I saw them. Bruce and LeDarius emerged from behind a large holly bush—so overgrown, it covered the entire corner of the house. My mom was constantly begging my dad to trim it. Today, I wished he would have done it.

The look in Bruce's eyes were different. There was no gleam of joy like he normally had when he would torture his prey. It sent chills down my spine. Also, one eye was swollen—no doubt it had come at the hands of his father based on what I had heard at lunch.

"Hey, faggot! You got me in trouble!"

At that, Bruce lunged at me, punching me in the face, chest, and stomach.

"Come on, LD. Get in here!" At this command, LeDarius joined in—kicking my legs. Soon, I was balled up against the side of the brick house just waiting for it to end. I felt like it went on for hours, but it was likely only a few minutes when I heard the blaring of a car horn and a man's voice.

"Hey, you little punk kids! I see you, Bruce and LeDarius. Get the hell out of here!" He was closer now—at my side pulling me to my feet. "Son, are you ok?"

I nodded my head in a haze. I really had no idea.

"I saw you this morning in the principal's office," said Mr. Antenelli. "What? You thought because you got in trouble, you'd come over here and get revenge? I've never seen such a despicable pair of boys in my life. I'll be calling both of your parents."

"So. Call them," Bruce said.

LeDarius looked terrified.

"Oh, I will. You rude little brat. Now, get out of here."

Bruce turned slowly and sauntered off with a smirk on his face while LeDarius hung his head—like a weary solider heading back into war.

"Come on, Imari. Grab your things."

I scooped up my bag and jacket and headed towards Mr. Antenelli's car. As we drove up to their home, Andrea, seemingly sensing something was different about her father's arrival, was waiting at the front door. When she saw me emerge from the car, she rushed towards us.

"Dad? Imari? What's going on?" As she asked the question, she could already see my disheveled and torn clothes and new bruises forming on my face.

"Imari, what happened?"

Mr. Antenelli interrupted. "Honey, go tell your mom we're going to have one more for dinner. Would you?"

"Ok." Andrea turned, face filled with concern, and headed back to the house.

"Come on, son. Let's have a chat."

We entered the den and Mr. Antenelli loosened his tie and poured himself a drink. "Can I get you something to drink?"

I looked up, concerned, thinking he meant alcohol. My mother certainly wouldn't approve of that. My father, on the other hand...

Realizing my confusion, Mr. Antenelli laughed. "No, no. Not alcohol. We have sodas and water here in this mini fridge."

"Oh," I said smiling, then immediately realizing my lip was split and wincing with pain. "Thank you, sir. Yes. A Coke if you have it?"

"We do. I'll get you a straw. That might be easier. Look here," he said as he popped open the soda. "If you move this bit all the way forward, it will hold your straw."

"Wow. I didn't know that!"

"Have a seat." I sat down on the couch adjacent

to his lounger. At this, he smiled and said, "Smart choice. Now, tell me what's been going on with those two."

Before I could even think to stop myself, it all came spilling out. I was not going to cry in front of him. Every time there was a catch in my throat, I stopped for a few seconds and took a sip from my Coke.

"That's a lot, Imari. What does your dad say about all this?"

At this, I looked down and shrugged my shoulders.

"He doesn't know, does he?" I shook my head. "Well, we'll have to tell him."

"Please don't, Mr. Antenelli. He'll only tell me that this is all my fault because I'm not fighting back."

"Yeah. I guess you're right. He didn't really seem too concerned when I spoke to him this morning. Well, this is not your fault, but you definitely need to fight back, son. Do you know how to fight?"

"No sir."

"Right. Stand up. Let me teach you a few moves that should help." As we both stood up, we heard Mrs. Antenelli's voice.

"Andrea, go to your room and stop eavesdropping."

"But Mom—"

"Don't 'but Mom' me. Now! And what are you two doing? Oh gosh, Imari, dear. What happened to you?"

"Those awful children, Bruce and LeDarius. Honey, we need to call their parents. Do you have that directory we got at the beginning of the school year?"

"Yes. I'll go get it. But what are you two doing?"

"I'm teaching Imari a few moves, so he can protect himself. He needs—"

"You will not! Imari, you come with me so I can clean you up."

I was frozen when Mr. Antenelli said with a smile in his eyes, "You better go. She's in charge around here."

After Mrs. Antenelli cleaned me up, she went down to my house and gathered a few things for me—clothing, my toothbrush, and sleeping bag before my father got home. She'd said that she left a note for him on the kitchen table. He wouldn't even notice I was missing, I'd said to her.

Once dinner was done, Mr. Antenelli pulled me downstairs to finish our fighting lesson. He said that the element of surprise was most important when dealing with bullies or when you were fighting more than one person.

"There are four moves I want you to focus on. First, and perhaps the most effective, is a kick to the balls. Maybe this won't hurt you boys as much now, but it's good to have this one handy anyway."

He then showed me how to load up my weight with my right foot in the back and transfer that weight forward—kicking his hand.

"Good, good. The important thing here, Imari, is to be the first person to strike. Now, the second move

I want you to focus on is a punch to the neck. No one ever sees this coming. And you want to aim right here in the middle at the base of the neck."

I did a few shadow punches, aiming at Mr. Antenelli's windpipe.

"Yep. Just like that. Great. Now, the third area is the nose. It bleeds easily and when someone is covered in blood, it's shocking for them. Depending on your location, you'll use a different method. If you're close, use the palm of your hand and ram it up, hitting the nose from underneath. If you have them bent over in pain, then grab the back of their head, and use your knee. Like this," he said, demonstrating both moves. I followed suit.

"Finally, sweep the leg. You put your right leg behind them and push hard. They will fall to the ground. You get on top of them and pin them, making sure your knees pin their arms to their side. Then, just start wailing on them." He demonstrated the move and I tried it on him a few times.

"Now, you could use these in combination. For example, you could start with a punch to the throat. Then, a kick to the balls. Knee them in the nose and sweep the leg, jump on them, and start pounding. Try it. But be careful around the balls, would you?" he said, laughing. And we went through the choreographed dance over and over until it started to feel natural.

"I think you've got it, son. Now, you just have to

summon the courage to use it in the moment. Look, you might as well. Even if you lose, you'll know you at least tried to fight back, and you can take pride in that."

"Yes sir. I will. And thank you. For everything."

"You're very welcome. Now, head back upstairs and see Mrs. Antenelli. She'll have your pajamas. We'll need to redress that wound of yours too."

Once I showered, I left my bandage off to give the wound some air. Mrs. Antenelli said she would redress it in the morning before school as long as I could sleep on my stomach. In Andrea's room, we talked through the day. Well, mostly Andrea talking. Then, we heard raised voices.

"Well, your son has no business in our neighborhood, terrorizing our children. It is certainly your problem! Perhaps if you spent less time drinking and more time with your son.... Well, I certainly see where your son gets his horrible attitude."

Andrea and I snuck down the hallway to listen.

"Jesus! What a piece of shit."

"What did he say?" Mrs. Antenelli asked.

"Well, he certainly didn't appreciate me interrupting his drinking. He said I should 'mind yo own business, white boy' and to 'stay out of black folks' business.' I certainly didn't know what he meant by that. I mean, it's no wonder Bruce is such a horrible child. At least LeDarius' mother was concerned. I think she was actually hitting him with the phone while we were on it."

"Oh my. That's awful."

"I feel no sympathy for that awful child. She said that it was her copier at her hair salon that they'd used to make that awful picture of Imani."

"Poor, sweet Imari. Why is it that the children with the most beautiful hearts are always tormented so much as children?"

"I don't know, honey. But I do know that we are all that boy has. I'm not sure why his extended family hasn't stepped in. Andrea said he even has a cousin in the same grade who has just stopped talking to him altogether."

"How strange."

"Yeah. Well, I intend to take him under my wing. Let him help me with stuff around the house—just so he knows he's not alone."

"I think that's lovely, honey. I know he'll be grateful for that."

At this, I turned and walked back to Andrea's room with tears running down my face. Andrea tried to talk to me, but I was shutting down. That worm of an idea started to reemerge—much stronger now. All the things that have happened to me—even the kindness I'd just heard from Mr. Antenelli, I only heard one thing. *There is something wrong with you. What's wrong with you that your family doesn't want anything to do with you? Your own cousin won't talk to you. Play cousin or not. This is all my fault.*

I fell asleep with tears still running down my face.

MARY

"I think that's lovely, honey. I know he'll be grateful for that," I said to Andrew.

"I feel like it's the best we can do for now. At least until the attorney contacts us. Did Imani tell you his name?"

"He's with one of those big firms in Atlanta, I think. Let me go find the business card. She told me she found his information in the paper. Here it is, Jason Delloqua. Mary asked me to reach out to him if the worst happened. When I spoke to him, he said he was sending a certified letter to George that outlines Mary's wishes and includes the letter she wrote to him. I'm not sure when they'll deliver it though since he needs to be there to sign for it."

"Maybe they already tried to deliver it."

"Yeah. Maybe."

"He didn't mention it when I spoke to him this morning. Honestly, honey, I think he's eager to no longer be responsible for Imari—not like he's ever really been responsible for him."

"Well, his loss. He doesn't deserve him."

"Damn right!"

17

IMARI

That morning at the Antenellis was great even though I was back in my funk. The bus ride was calm and peaceful. I sat in the back of the bus just because I wanted to get the most enjoyment of Bruce and LeDarius being out of school for as long as I could.

When we arrived at school, I stopped by Nurse Rangles office as she made me promise I would swing by each morning for a while until the stitches were removed. I saw the concern on her face as soon as I entered her office.

"Dear God. What has happened to you now?"

I simply shrugged my shoulders.

"I really shouldn't say this, Imari, but you're going to have to start fighting back. You don't deserve to be treated this way."

I immediately discounted this. While I understood that she was coming from a good place, she was wrong. I absolutely did deserve this. If I were a normal boy, none of this would be happening to me.

"Imari. Don't you believe that you deserve to be treated better?"

"No ma'am. I don't."

At this Nurse Rangles teared up. "Well, you're wrong. You're a sweet, beautiful boy with a kind heart and you deserve love and respect and true friendship."

When Nurse Rangles finished addressing wounds, old and new, I made my way to my homeroom class.

"Geez, Imari. Every day it's a new injury with you. Are you in some street fighting gang?" Mr. Smith joked.

I simply walked past him to my seat. My seat that did not have Bruce in my direct line of sight. That was a silver lining.

The rest of the school day was uneventful. The way school should be. When we arrived at our bus stop, I told Andrea I wanted to spend some time alone at the pond. She said she would let her mom know and to not be too long.

The grass around the pond had started to turn brown. The lilies had also started to wither. They'd be back in the spring. The ducks, too, had taken off for warmer weather. This seemed like an appropriate scene to match how I felt inside—desolate and in desperate need of light and warmth. Then, I felt something large hit me in the back of the head. A rock. Throbbing pain soared through my head. I reached back. My head was slippery wet and I pulled back a crimson-stained hand. When I turned around, I saw Bruce there alone.

"Hey faggot. Yo little white master tried to get me in trouble with my ol' man. He didn't give a shit though, did he," he said laughing.

I slowly got to my feet and started trying to put more distance between the two of us. I remembered the old, abandoned shed and took off running.

"You can't outrun me, faggot," he said—laughing maniacally. "I can't fucking wait to catch you."

I rounded the corner of the shed and forced my way in and closed the door. I'd never been in here before. There appeared to be some old farm tools rusted from many years of neglect. I tried to position an old wheelbarrow in front of the door but I wasn't fast enough and Bruce kicked in the door.

"Nowhere to run now, E-dead mommy. Maybe if I beat yo ass hard enough, you can see her again." He slowly started to step towards me.

The element of surprise. I reached back and threw my punch at his throat. While surprised indeed, I missed my target and Bruce just laughed.

"Oh good. You gonna fight back. Dat will make dis ass-whoppin' even betta."

He kicked me hard in the center of my chest and sent me flying backwards—my head colliding against something hard and metal. I immediately fell to the floor. Bruce laughed as he kicked me, over and over. As I was losing consciousness, I heard him say, "I'm not stopping this time until you're dead. I fucking hate you."

When I awoke, someone was calling my name.

"Imari! Where are you?" Andrea asked. "Imari!"

I couldn't move and, furthermore, I didn't want to. I just laid back down and went back to sleep. As I was sleeping, the last few moments of my fight with Bruce came clearly into view. I was sure Bruce was going to kill me. He'd said as much. Maybe I would still die and maybe that was ok. I had no fight left in me. I could feel myself negotiating with God—praying that he take me up to heaven to be safe again in the arms of my mother.

When I woke again, I was being carried by Mr. Antenelli. He placed me in the back of his car. I wondered if this was some weird dream—like the ones I was having of my mom. Was she going to show up here soon and let me join in her adventure?

When I woke again, I was in a hospital room and my father was at the foot of my bed.

"You awake, boy?"

I sat up. I couldn't remember the last time I'd actually spoken to my father.

"Where am I?"

"You're in the hospital, costing me a lot of damn money. Let me grab a nurse so we can get you out of here."

When my father returned, it was with the doctor.

"Imari. How are you feeling? Your father says you're asking to go home," the doctor said.

I could see my father behind the doctor giving me a very stern eye. I knew what he wanted me to say but I honestly didn't care anymore what happened to me. "I didn't say that."

"What, boy? Don't lie to this doctor. Now, here's your clothes. Get dressed and let's get out of here."

"Mr. Johnson, if I may, your son has had several serious head traumas over the past few days. We really should keep him here for observation. If you leave, you'd have to sign him out against medical advice."

"Fine. Where do I sign?"

"Mr. Johnson. You—"

"Give me the paper and let me sign. I can't afford this. Now, unless you want to use yo doctor's salary to pay for this, I'd suggest you mind yo business. I know how to take care of this boy." Then to me, "Put your clothes on. Now."

The doctor left the room, shaking his head and mumbling something under his breath. The nurse returned with paperwork for my father to sign. He snatched the papers from her and scribbled his signature quickly and tossed it back at her.

"Let's go."

When I got to my feet, I stumbled a little. I was still in a bit of a haze. As we made our way through the ward out to the waiting room, there were the Antenellis. At the sight of me, Andrea ran forward to give me a hug but stopped short when my father grabbed my arm, pulling me towards the exit.

"George, please wait," Mr. Antenelli pleaded but my father just kept moving forward through the front doors of the emergency room. I didn't dare look back. In fact, I was afraid that if I did, I might lose my balance. I heard the doors close behind me. I wasn't sure if the Antenellis were looking on or not.

At the car, my father backhanded me hard across the face, knocking me into the side of the car. I was too defeated at this point to even care.

"Oh, you thought you were gonna show yo ass in front of dem white people with no consequences? I don't give a damn who did this to you. If you ever disrespect me again, I'll take you out."

I stumbled around to the passenger side of the car and got in the back seat and immediately laid down. I was so tired. As I was falling asleep, I caught snippets of my father still spewing his anger.

"Such a punk...probably deserved...can't believe you, my son...wish you were never born...can't wait to be rid of you."

As I drifted off to sleep, I prayed. Please, God, let me sleep forever.

Hours later I believe or maybe days later, I woke up still in the back of my father's car. I stepped out into the darkness, confused. It was the time of the early, early morning where even the birds were sleeping, and the sounds of the cicadas filled the air. I walked to the front door and went to open it when I realized it was locked. I couldn't believe it. Then the events of the day came rushing back to me. The abandoned shed, the hospital, the run in with the doctor, Mr. Antenelli, the awful things my father had said. "I wish you were never born." I searched my pockets, but I didn't have my key to the house. What had I done with it? I would have had it with me when I went to the pond. Then I remembered that I was in a hospital gown at the hospital. My father must have taken my key from me. What was I going to do? I could go back and sleep in the back of my father's car but the thought of that made me angry. I didn't want anything from this man anymore—not even shelter.

When I arrived at the Antenellis' door, it was Mr. Antenelli who answered with a baseball bat in his hand, wearing a t-shirt and underwear.

"Who's there?" Then, realizing it was me, he softened his tone. "Imari, son. What are you doing out here? Did you sneak out of your house? Your father—"

"Left me in the back of his car and locked the front door."

I could see the blood boil in Mr. Antenelli's eyes. He was gripping the bat so tightly, his knuckles were turning white.

"Andrew, honey, who is it?"

"Go back to sleep, sweetheart. It's just Imari." At this, Mrs. Antenelli came flying around the corner in her nightgown. Her hair flowing around her shoulders.

"Oh God. Imari, what are you doing here?"

"His father left him in the back of the car, honey, and locked him out."

She turned her head and said something under her breath.

"Well, fortunately, we still have your sleeping bag here and clothes for a few days. Go and brush your teeth, dear, and I'll set up your sleeping bag for you. Are you in any pain?"

I thought about this for a second. Pain is all I felt. My lip, face, back of the head but most of all, deep inside my soul. I nodded.

"Ok. I'll get you something to help with the pain and something to help you get some sleep."

I finished brushing my teeth and Mrs. Antenelli met me at the door with a couple of pills to take. I was at the age where you just didn't question when an adult handed you medicine to take—unless it was that disgusting pink stuff. I took the pills and made my way into Andrea's room and slid into my sleeping bag. Mrs. Antenelli knelt down, pulling her hair around to one side of her head while placing a kiss on my forehead.

"Good night, Imari. Sleep tight, ok?"

"Ok."

MARY

I was always told that God would never give you more than you can handle. But in the case of Imari, this felt like an untruth. How much could this child go through in such a short period of time? I'd also heard about how cruel children can be, but I had never witnessed anything like this before in my life. All I wanted was to honor the promise I had made to Imani to take care of her son. She must be so disappointed in us. Had she made the wrong choice? And while it didn't matter to us that Imari was black, I know that other people wouldn't see it the same way. White saviors, they'll call us. But Imani was my friend and she trusted me to take care of her son. I had to believe that we could give him a better life that his own father could. He clearly hated his son. Imani had suggested that George despised his son because of the relationship she had with Imari.

"He's jealous," she'd said to me.

"Well, if he wants to have a better relationship with you, he should stop being such an asshole and treat you better."

We'd both laughed at that. God, I missed her. It was so unfair that we got such a short time to be together. She was such an amazing woman.

Well, I was going to do right by her son. I was going to do all I could to make him feel loved and protected.

18

IMARI

I was awakened by the smell of bacon and Jeffrey's laughter in the distance. I couldn't remember if it was the weekend or a school morning. Judging by the amount of light in the room, it was well past the time I would normally leave for school. Andrea's bed was made and her bookbag was gone. I got up and made my way down the hall to the bathroom. I got dressed and walked toward the smell of the bacon, realizing that I had not eaten anything since lunch at school the prior day.

"Imari. Come, sweetheart. I thought the smell of bacon might wake you. You must be starving!"

I tried to summon a smile, but it wouldn't reach my face. Playing in a loop in my head were my father's words—wishing me away and then leaving me in the back of the car like some old, discarded piece of trash. But then, that's exactly what I was.

"I've phoned the school and they know you're going to be out for the rest of the week. I also spoke to Nurse Rangles and she's going to pop by on her lunch break to check on you."

I nodded my head as I crammed breakfast down my mouth. My overwhelming desire to quench my hunger tapped into the part of me that wanted to be alive. I couldn't go on like this anymore. I had tried to fight back and made things worse. But I had relied on a weakness in a time of distress instead of my strength. My mother's words from the side of the pond came rushing back to me.

"If you learn from your mistakes, then you've made the most of it. It's the best way to learn really."

I have learned, Mom. I should never have tried to use force to overcome my enemy.

This time, I would use my cunning and wit to lure him into my trap. He needed to understand what it was like to live in fear—if only for a moment. I needed to be convincing and would have to pull from the darkness within me. I was going to end this, once and for all.

19

IMARI

A few weeks had passed, and I was back in school. Mrs. Antenelli had taken to driving me and Andrea to school and picking us up in her minivan. I could tell that it was a lot for her to do, packing up Jeffrey each time, making sure we were both ready for school. I was living with the Antenellis full time now. I wasn't sure for how much longer. Surely, they would tire of me sooner or later.

At school, because Bruce and LeDarius had been suspended for their bullying and it was widely known what Bruce had done to me outside of school, the teachers had intervened, making sure the chances of our interactions was very small. There were moments where I thought that this might be enough to assuage my fear of another attack. He had been clear though. He intended to kill me. Was I just supposed to sit around and wait for this to happen? I wished my mom was here. It would have been hard to talk to her about this but I would have, I think. I couldn't talk to the Antenellis. They have done enough for me already. I couldn't burden them with this too. Maybe I could talk to Nurse Rangles. She was always so kind to me and seemed genuinely interested in my well-being. But when I thought about bringing this up to her, I couldn't imagine having the courage to do it. No. I was going to have to handle this myself and doing nothing was not an option. I didn't want to die at the hands of this bully. After all the horrible things he'd done to me and said about my mother, I would not let him take my life too. The more I considered this thought, the angrier I got. Anger was turning into resentment to the point that every time I heard his laugh or saw his face, I found myself clinching my fist and my jaw. I did not want to live in this fear anymore. I was going to make him pay for what he had put me through. It was him or me.

I needed materials for my plan to work and I needed time away from the prying eyes of the Antenellis to do it. I would tell them I wanted to spend some time outside alone. Mrs. Antenelli seemed very sympathetic to this while also being very concerned. The last time I had ventured out alone, I ended up in the emergency room. Andrea, however, seemed very hurt by this. I tried to assure her that this had nothing to do with her, but she never really seemed to believe me.

I had very small windows of time to get the materials I needed. The side door to our garage was the pathway to all I needed. My father never built anything anymore, so I was certain he wouldn't miss any of the things I took from him. First though, I needed to get in and take an inventory of what was available. My father had never really taught me much that I found useful except this one thing. There was a trick to getting into the side door without a key, but I'd need a flathead screwdriver. Fortunately, Mr. Antenelli had taken me under his wing and was showing me how to fix things around the house. One of those times, I had stolen away one of his flatheads. He had many more so I was hoping he wouldn't miss this one.

I jimmied my way into the garage, turned on the light, and started looking around. One by one, I started pulling the items I needed out of the garage and around to the back of the house, placing them under the plastic tarp used to cover the firewood. I would have to come back at night to do most of the work, but I would need as much time as possible to dig the hole. As it was getting colder, it wasn't odd to see me with a large coat on. I put the handle of the shovel down the side of my pants leg but at ten years old, I was still too short to hide the head of shovel under my coat. I'd have to find another way. I walked across the street, through the trail, around the pond to the shed, and started to have a look around. Surveying the shed in earnest for the first time, I realized there was a lot of what I needed already here. This certainly made things easier. Most importantly, there was a shovel.

Digging was much harder than I thought. The ground was getting colder, making it harder to work, but each time I started to tire, I saw the picture Bruce and LeDarius made of my mother and I would dig harder. As I was digging, I would come across worms, and I would save them in one of the old plastic buckets that were there. I needed to create something like quicksand. There was a very old bag of some sort of seed. I combined that seed with mud and water from the pond. I stuck my hand down in it. It wasn't quite thick enough. I kept playing around with the formula until it was right. I had to keep feeding it water each day so that it wouldn't harden, which would make it completely unusable.

After three weeks, I was ready for the final steps in my plan. This was going to require some trickery. Since I had been staying with the Antenellis, Jeffrey had been staying in the room with his parents as I shared a room with Andrea. Their downstairs was still unfinished, but they had poured a concrete floor. There were a few windows and a sliding glass door that led out to the side of the house. At dinner that night, I started to lay out my plan.

"Mr. Antenelli, the downstairs is starting to look nice."

Lighting up at the prospect of talking about something he was actually interested in, he said, "Yes. Still a long way to go of course. But with the floor leveled and the insulation done, we're getting there. Might move my den down there."

"You'll do no such thing! You promised me a walk-in closet, honey."

"Of course, dear," Mr. Antenelli said, winking at me.

"Before you finish things, it would be a cool place to spend the night. Like a camp out but inside." As I said this, I looked over at Andrea to gauge her interest. She jumped on board right away.

"Oh yes. Please, Daddy."

"Ah, I can't say no to that face."

"She's got you wrapped around her little finger, Andrew," Mrs. Antenelli said with what seemed to be the smallest tinge of jealousy. Mr. Antenelli nodded in agreement and smiled.

After dinner, Mr. Antenelli and I laid down some mats between two posts downstairs, tied a rope between the posts, and draped a large white sheet over it. He taped down the corners with duct tape. I did really enjoy spending time with Mr. Antenelli and appreciated that he took the time to actually teach me things. I felt bad for deceiving him, but it was necessary. The last part of my plan would require the veil of night.

That night, Andrea and I told ghost stories using large flashlights. This was my idea. I would need a flashlight tonight. We played card and board games late into the night before Andrea started to get sleepy. Soon she was asleep, and the waiting game began. I needed to be sure the rest of my neighbors had also laid down for the night and I was a few hours away from that. I was fighting sleep myself, so I sat up in my sleeping bag, trying to nurture the buzz of nervousness and excitement coursing through me.

It was time. I had insisted that I bring my clothes down with me. Mrs. Antenelli didn't balk too much at this. I slipped on my clothes and grabbed my flashlight and headed toward the sliding door. Mr. Antentelli had shown me where the key was and how to remove the bar there as a security measure. I walked over to where the key was hanging and unlocked the door. As I went to remove the bar, it was stuck. "Shit!" I said to myself. It was so important that I be as quiet as possible. If Andrea caught me, there'd be no way to explain this. I had thought about saying I was sleep-walking but that didn't really seem plausible as I had been sleeping in her room for weeks without doing this. No. I would need to be quiet.

With a little more leverage, I pushed hard on the bar, knocking it loose and dropping the keys on the hard concrete floor. *No!* I thought. I'm done for now.

In the silence, the sound seemed to reverberate throughout the house. I stood completely still, willing Andrea not to wake up. I stayed that way for what felt like several minutes before I relaxed. If Andrea had woken up, she would have certainly noticed I was gone and would be up and looking around for me.

I placed the security bar up against the wall in a way that I was sure it wouldn't fall and slid the door open. I was immediately hit by the cold night air that made me shiver all over. I fought the urge to audibly express my shock. I slowly slid the door closed and tiptoed around the side of the Antenellis' house.

Other than the streetlights, the neighborhood was dark. I didn't see any lights on in any bedroom windows as I slithered from around the side of the house across the dew-filled front yard down the hill to my house. I made my way around the back of the house and lifted the tarp. I used the sheers to cut away a few feet of the tarp toward the back where it wouldn't be missed and grabbed the red plastic gas can. Once I was behind the dogwood at the start of the trail, I turned on my flashlight and made my way to the old shed. I grabbed one of the empty buckets and filled it with wood scraps and doused them with gasoline. Then I took my tarp piece and used it to cover the hole that was in the center of the dirt floor of the shed. I then lightly dusted it with dirt and old pine needles, trying to make it blend in with rest of the floor. At last, my trap was set. Now, I just needed to lure my prey.

ANDREW

It was so great having Imari around full time now. He was always so respectful and inquisitive. But lately, he'd seem distracted and detached. I would make sure to pull him outside as much as possible—throwing a ball with him, telling him about my favorite sports teams and how me and my dad would go to baseball games when I was a kid and how I'd love to take him to one in Atlanta.

Mary and I had told our parents that we were planning to adopt Imari. My parents were living back in Italy but thought it was an amazing thing we were doing. Mary's parents though—they expressed concern.

"Are you sure you want to burden yourself with someone else's child?" Mary's mom had said.

"He's not someone else's child, Mom. He's ours. The only thing that remains is paperwork. But he's already our son and all I'm interested in hearing from you is your support." I'd loved that response from Mary. Yes. Imari was already our son, and I was so proud to be his father.

I knew there were going to be challenges of course. There was no ignoring the fact that we were living in the South, raising a black son. Even though we were twenty years past the Civil Rights movement, many people were going to have their opinion about it and Imari would struggle with things that we would never truly understand. But I intended to make it my duty to learn everything I could and make sure he never felt like he needed to deny his heritage to fit into this family.

For now, I just needed to make sure he got as much attention from me as possible. He was starving for it and I could tell he was struggling—detaching. I thought maybe that this was his way of dealing with losing his mother and his father abandoning him. Is that what it felt like for him, that his father was abandoning him? Or was he happy to be out of that house and away from him?

When we were working on chores or outside throwing the ball, I would try to encourage him to talk about how things were going. We hadn't told him yet about what was going on legally with us adopting him. Mary and I had decided that it was best to wait until we had crossed all hurdles and it was certain to go through before we brought it up to him or the other kids. Jeffrey wouldn't really understand, and Andrea would be delighted. But I couldn't get him to open up. Maybe he was worried that we were going to send him back home to his father if he complained or overshared. I just wished I knew what was going on in that head of his.

It was then that I started to notice that he was going into the woods by himself. I knew that there was a pond back in those woods that he would go to with his mom, so it made sense that he was going there. And I didn't want to intrude on this memory. This was obviously something that meant a great deal to him and probably connected him to his mother, which was a good thing. He needed that. So, I would slyly watch as he would go into the woods and would follow at a distance. I got turned around the first time I followed him in and was afraid I was going to run into him. He'd feel like his trust was violated. I couldn't let that happen. When I found the opening to the pond, I didn't see him there. There was a small abandoned shed off in the distance and there seemed to be some noise coming from it. There was no way for me to get any closer though without risking running into him, so I just waited.

When he was finished, I hid off the path and waited for him to pass. As he was walking by me, he turned and looked around. Shit! Had he spotted me? But he quickly kept walking and disappeared into the trail. When I was certain that he was out of earshot and sight, I made my way to the shed. I think I was expecting to see some sort of shrine to his mother. Instead, I saw a shovel and a hole and other tools. I didn't really think much of it. As a boy, my friends and I would always dig and build things in the woods. I just wished he had friends to do this with instead of coming out here by himself. Perhaps he just needed some place that was just his where he knew belonged to him. If so, that made sense to me.

20

IMARI

I had given thought to the best way of getting Bruce to the shed. In the end, I decided that I needed to find a time to catch him alone. While that was difficult in the past, LeDarius' mother had forbidden him from spending time with Bruce while in school. As such, Bruce was alone quite often but rarely alone out of sight of teachers. There were really only a few times a day where I would have a chance. I would either have to catch him in the restroom or on the playground during recess. The first option would require a bit of luck while the second option had all sorts of logistical hurdles. In the end, it happened in an entirely different way.

The lunch line snaked into the kitchen, through one door. You'd pick up your tray and tell the lunch lady what you were having that day, then leave through another door back to the cafeteria tables. I reached down to pick up my tray when someone knocked it out of my hand. I turned to see Bruce standing there. We were the last two people in the line. The kitchen was loud. Machines running, cafeteria workers talking loudly. No one could hear the conversation we would have.

"Hey, faggot. Thought you could get away from me, huh?"

This was my moment. Time to lay the bait.

"The only reason you won last time is because you caught me by surprise." I was careful not to be too eager, but the line was moving along. There were a few students ahead of us, but no one was really paying attention to us.

"Oh yeah, faggot? Let's go again right now then!"

"No. Not here. I don't want anyone around to break us up."

"Ok. When and where, punk?"

"Same place as last time. Today at 5 o'clock."

"Fine, faggot. I'll be there. You better not chicken out."

"I won't."

Back at the lunch table, Andrea said, "I saw that Bruce was behind you in line. Did he say anything to you?"

"No. Not a thing." I felt bad lying to Andrea and

the rest of the Antenellis. They had been so good to me. I had not given much thought to what would happen after today. If I managed to come out of the day alive, that's all that mattered to me.

The rest of the school day went by in a haze. I was certainly not present. Would my plan work? Had I thought through all the possible outcomes? I was brought back to the present at the sound of the end-of-day school bell. I gathered my things and stole a glance at Bruce. He punched his open palm in a display that was meant to provoke fear. I simply held his gaze for a few seconds and turned and walked out the door.

Mrs. Antenelli was there to pick us up at 3:30 p.m.

"Hello, hello. How was school today?" Jeffrey made a high-pitched squeal when he saw me.

Andrea answered and went on for a while about her day when her mother interrupted.

"Imari, it's time to get your stitches out. We're swinging by your doctor's office on the way home." She saw the look of concern on my face. "Oh, don't worry, dear. It won't hurt at all."

"Ok. Thanks. Do you know how long it will take?"

"Why? Have somewhere you need to be?" she said—laughing a little.

"No ma'am. Just wondering."

"Not sure, sweetheart. Not too long." This did

nothing to assuage the rising panic I felt. Of course this was going to happen today of all days. Couldn't have been yesterday.

It was 3:46 p.m. when we arrived at the doctor's office. Mrs. Antenelli checked me in and had to fill out some paperwork. When she finished, she sat down next to me, Andrea, and Jeffrey.

"Should only be a few minutes," Mrs. Antenelli said.

I was getting antsy. It was now 4:05 p.m. when the nurse called my name.

"Imari Johnson?"

"Yes. That's me." I jumped up and followed the nurse.

"Imari, do you want me to come with you?"

"No thanks, Mrs. Antenelli."

The nurse led me back to one of the rooms and I climbed up on the table. I had had to buzz my hair weeks ago and keep it that way. It was easier than walking around with a chunk of hair missing. Mr. Antenelli had done it for me.

"Ok, sweetheart. Let's see how you've been healing." She inspected my head. "Yes. Looks great. So, the doctor will be in shortly and he'll get those itchy stitches out of your head, ok?"

"Thank you."

I glanced down at my watch. It was 4:09 p.m. I

wasn't going to make it.

By 4:24 p.m., I was walking out of the doctor's office. We all jumped in the car and headed back home. I was bouncing in my seat—nervous energy coursing through my veins. Andrea was trying to carry on a conversation with me, but I just couldn't focus on what she was saying. Jeffrey also tried to get my attention to no avail.

When we arrived home at 4:36 p.m., I asked Mrs. Antenelli if I could go outside for a little while.

"Sure, sweetheart. Are you ok?"

"Yes, ma'am. I'm fine. I just want to spend some time alone." I said this while glancing at Andrea to make sure she'd heard the "alone" part. She had and looked sad.

I walked down the hill and through the trail to the old shack. What if Bruce had gotten there early? All my hard work would be ruined. In the end, I didn't need to worry. Bruce wasn't there so I got to work. I got some water from the pond and mixed it into the homemade quicksand I had distributed over three buckets. When it was the right consistency, I poured the mixture into the hole and covered the hole back up with my tarp. It was dark enough in this shed that I didn't really need to cover the tarp that well. I filled my three buckets that I used with for the quicksand with the pile of rocks I had been collecting for weeks. There were a lot of moving parts to this plan. I hoped that I would have the nerve and wherewithal to pull this off.

5:00 p.m. came and went. *He's not coming,* I thought. I can't believe I had gone through all this planning and effort just to be made a fool of again. I thought for sure that his ego would not allow him to turn this down. I decided that I would wait it out for fifteen more minutes before I abandoned the plan altogether. At 5:14 p.m., I started to gather my things to leave when the door to the shed opened. *Oh god. It's happening.* I was positioned opposite of the door with the tarp-covered hole between us.

"I'm really gonna enjoy this, E-dead Mommy. This time though, I'm not going to stop when I knock you out. You been practicing some more of your karate moves?" He laughed as he took a step inside the door.

"Your dad hit you anymore, bedwetter?" I said.

At this, Bruce lunged at me and let out an audible yelp as he fell into the deep and narrow hole. Quickly I grabbed the bucket of rocks and filled the hole around his knees and thighs. He was struggling to get out of the hole, but I was too fast. He clawed at the loose ground around him to no avail. He was stuck.

"You wait till I get out of here, faggot."

"But you're not getting out of here," I said—steely and cold. I didn't recognize the voice coming out of me. I had tapped into my despair and hopelessness. A chill cut through the shed as the temperature seemed to drop about ten degrees.

"Wha-at...?"

I grabbed the collection of worms I had saved and threw them on him. "I'm going to let them eat you." At this he seemed to let out a breath he'd been holding in for minutes.

"That's your big plan? You gonna let worms eat me? I was startin' to think you'd grown some balls. What a fucking punk. You have me trapped in a hole and all you do is throw a few worms on me." He laughed.

"But that's not all I'm going to do." Still in a very detached voice. "Those aren't the worms that are going to eat you." I turned and started to throw the gasoline-soaked logs into the hole.

Still laughing he said, "What? You gonna wait til some worms crawl under these logs? Seriously, E-dead Mommy. I thought you were smart. That picture I made was of yo dead momma in the ground being eaten by worms. Not like sitting on the sofa. Dead. And in the ground."

I had my back turned to him when I answered. "Yes. That's right." When I turned, I kept what I had in my hands behind my back.

Starting to get worried, Bruce nervously asked, "What? Yo gonna bury me alive?"

"No. That would take too long. You're going to die right now." I pulled the matchbox and match from behind my back. And held them up where he could see them. He must have then noticed the smell coming from the logs and started trying to remove them from the hole. I just kicked them back in and stuck the match.

"Wait! Don't! I'm sorry. Please. Don't!"

"Goodbye, you sorry piece of shit."

"Wait! Ok. Ok. I'm sorry. I was just playing around. Damn. You can't take a little joke?"

It's working, I thought. I had to make sure though. He had to believe that I was serious about hurting him. I went to throw the match on the soaked firewood.

"Fuck! Stop, Imari. Shit. What the fuck? Let me out of here, man. Ok. I'll leave you alone. It's not fun anymore anyway," he said with a pleading look in his eyes.

I stepped back, pretending to agonize over the decision. This is all I really wanted—for him to really be afraid that I could hurt him and to agree that he would stop hurting me. Believing that I was still considering dropping the match, Bruce continued to plead with me.

"Imari! Please don't do this!" he pleaded.

I continued to pretend to really consider his pleas for help. When I felt things were reaching a fever pitch, I pretended to relent.

"Ok," I said. "But this all ends here. No more talking about my mom. No more bullying. You leave me and my friends alone forever. You agree?"

"Yes. Yes. I'll leave you alone. I promise."

Convinced that I had finally gotten what I wanted, I went to the corner to grab the shovel. Bruce grabbed the end of the shovel and I pulled him out of the hole with a great deal of effort on both of our parts—sloshing noises filled the shed from the mud as Bruce tried to emerge from his death trap. I couldn't believe that this had worked. I had used my brain and it had served me well.

Once fully out of the hole, I dropped the shovel and took a step back to give Bruce room to leave the shed. But then his demeanor changed.

"You're so fucking stupid. You should have killed me when you had the chance, faggot."

Bruce grabbed the shovel and swung it at my knees. I jumped back just in time to avoid the first strike. Undeterred, he dropped the shovel and ran at me, tackling me to the ground. This was never going to end. He was right. I was stupid to think that this would work. We rolled around on the ground, both fighting to get the upper hand but then he got on top of me, straddling my chest with his knees pinning my shoulders to the cold dirt. He saw the box of matches on the ground and reached for them. As he did, I struggled to get off from under him, but I couldn't manage to push him away.

"Thanks for the idea. Setting you on fire here is perfect. People will probably just think this was an accident. No one even knows I'm here."

Of course this was how it would end for me. Again, I had tried to fight back and had lost. But I would not go down without a fight. Not this time. My hands were exploring the dirt from my position on the ground, and my hand landed on a piece of wood. Without thinking, I gripped my hand around it and hit Bruce in the back with all the force I could muster in that position. He yelped in pain and jumped up, trying to grab the piece of wood still hanging from his back. I realized then that there must have been some nails in that piece of wood.

I quickly jumped up and lunged at him and punched him in the throat. Shocked and gasping for air, Bruce stepped back and fell in the hole. I started to notice the smell of smoke. Bruce must have struck a match right before I hit him. I saw the gas can in the corner knocked over and spilling gas everywhere. It was happening so fast, but I could see it all frame by frame. The pine needles on the ground, igniting and making its way to the spilled gasoline. The gas igniting and soon engulfing the red, plastic gas container. I was so mesmerized by the flame; I'd almost forgotten Bruce was there until I felt rocks hitting me. Bruce had started throwing them at me to get my attention.

"Let me out of here, you faggot! I'm going to fucking kill you."

I went to take a step toward him but reconsidered. This was never going to stop. If I let him out of this hole, he would certainly try to kill me. Bruce seemed to see me work this out in my head, but he was too angry to try pleading anymore.

"You get me out of here now or I'm going to fuck you up, faggot. Now!"

I slowly stepped back towards the door to the shed.

"You better not leave me in here! If I get out of here, I'm going to fucking kill you! You hear me, faggot. You're fucking dead."

"This isn't what I wanted. Why couldn't you just leave me alone?"

I closed the door to the shed and walked away toward the pond. The farther I got, the more difficult it was to hear Bruce' screams for help. Soon, the shed was fully engulfed in flames. I sat on the edge of the pond and waited.

That was where I stayed. It was hard to smell anything but smoke. I was wondering how deep the pond was when I heard a noise behind me.

"Imari? Imari, son. What's going on? Did I hear screaming?"

I turned to see Mr. Antenelli, his face filled with intense worry. Slowly, I pointed at the burning shed.

"Fuck. Fuck. Is someone in there?" He ran towards the shed.

This was not how this was supposed to end. I could not believe I managed to mess this up. I heard Mr. Antenelli knocking in the front door of the shed.

Everything I touch turns to shit. That's it. I'm done

trying. I had decided that today was going to be the day I finally took control of what was happening to me. I needed this to stop today. I couldn't convince Bruce to stop but there was one other way this could all end. I slowly got up from the side of the pond and walked into the water. It was colder than I thought it would be but that didn't deter me. Soon, the water was up to my chin, and I let myself sink down into the muddy waters—my skin like a piece of dark chocolate melting into a cup of hot cocoa.

As I continued to sink, I closed my eyes and gave into the pull of my despair. I wasn't scared. I knew that I would be with my mother again soon.

21

IMARI

When I woke up, I was soaked and sitting in the front seat of Mr. Antenelli's car, confused about how I got there. Did I dream what had happened? The last thing I remembered was walking into the pond and allowing myself to be pulled beneath the water. I had thought I remembered rolling onto my back as I sank and seeing a bright light—warm and welcoming. I went to reach for that light when everything went dark. Suddenly, I coughed up some water.

"Imari, son. Are you ok? Fuck, you had me so fucking worried. Jesus—fuck." I had never heard the F-word used so many times in one sentence. I was then startled by more coughing coming from the back seat. I turned to see Bruce covered in soot in the backseat, but he was out of it. Suddenly I noticed an intense burn on my right hand. It was starting to blister. I hadn't noticed this earlier. I must have burned it on the way out of the shed.

"Fuck. Fuck. Fuck. Jesus. What the fuck, Imari?" Mr. Antenelli said—his hands shaking on the steering wheel. "I can't believe—were you trying to kill him, Imari?"

I couldn't answer. He wouldn't understand anyway.

"Imari, I need you to answer me honestly, ok? Why did you do that? Were you trying to hurt him?" Mr. Antenelli asked a little softer this time—trying to coax an answer out of me the way you might try to persuade an abused animal out of a corner.

"Look, Imari. You're going to need to start talking. I feel like I don't know you anymore. You have always been such a sweet kid to my daughter, and I've seen the way these boys have bullied you. But murder? Imari, that's a big fucking leap. Now, you're going to need to start talking or after I drop this kid off at the emergency room, I'll be making another stop at the police station."

I was still disoriented and was having a difficult time trying to pull my words together, but I could see something new in Mr. Antenelli's eyes. What was it? Was it fear? The realization came of what he must be thinking: *Do I have a killer in my car?* Well, he certainly did, but it wasn't me. But jail? Was I willing to go to jail for this? I hadn't really thought this all the way through. I just felt like I didn't have any other choice and now, I was going to need to convince Mr. Antenelli of this or this was going to be the end of me.

"Mr. Antenelli, I know what you must be thinking—how it must look." I swallowed hard finding it difficult to find my voice. "I know you know what's been happening with Bruce. Things just kept getting worse. He just wouldn't stop—was never going to stop. And after the last time, he said he was going to kill me. I didn't feel like I had any other choice but to fight back. I had just brought him to the shed to try and scare him into leaving me alone but when I let him out of the hole, he attacked me, and I knew it was going to be him or me. He was never going to leave me alone."

"Yes. Ok. But murder. There are so many steps between being threatened and retaliating with murder." Each time he used the word murder it felt like a punch in the gut.

"I didn't try to murder him—just scare him. He's the one who lit the match that started the fire. I didn't know what else to do. If my mom was still here..." Tears flooded my eyes. *What have I done?* She would be so disappointed in what I'd done—in who I had become. Both hands went up to cover my face as I began to sob uncontrollably.

"Ok, son," Mr. Antenelli said taking one hand off the steering wheel and caressing the back of my head. "I know you felt like you didn't have any options. I don't know what it's like to lose a parent at your age, especially one as amazing as Imani. I'm sure you must have felt cornered. And maybe if your mom was still here, she would have done a better job than we have been able to do to get you through this. This is really hard for all of us. But I can see how remorseful you are and that's the boy I know and have seen over these past few months. You have to understand though, Imari. Nothing like this can ever happen again. You understand me? You are going to have to talk to someone when you are having difficult times and don't know what to do. You can't make these types of drastic decisions. You're too young to understand perspective. Everything that happens to you, you think that's going to be your life forever."

I was listening intently and had managed to stop crying. I took a chance to glance over at Mr. Antenelli as he was keeping his eyes on the road, still rushing to the hospital but looking over occasionally to see if this was sinking in.

"Imari. Do you understand me? Never again."

I considered this. It was so different to have a man, a father, who asked me questions and believed me when I answered them. I could tell that he meant what he said—that I could come to him. *Why couldn't this man be my father?* I thought and suddenly felt very jealous of Andrea.

"I promise. Never again," I said.

"Good," Mr. Antenelli said as a weight was seemingly lifted from his shoulders. I could see the wheels turn as he immediately shifted his train of thought. "Listen, Imari. Here's the story we're going to tell at the hospital. Son? Are you listening?"

Confused, I nodded.

"You saw smoke coming from the shed and heard screams for help. You tried to get in when you burned your hand on the flames. You ran back to the pond to dip your burned hand in water when you slipped and fell in. You got out of the pond and ran to get help when you saw me driving by. You brought me to the shed, and I rescued Bruce. The story will be that Bruce had come here to ambush you in the shed and set you on fire."

"But—"

"But nothing, Imari. That's what happened. Now, repeat it back to me."

"I, I saw smoke...I heard screams. Umm—"

"Come on! We don't have a lot of time."

His urgency sobered me up. He was trying to help me, and I needed to try hard to get this right.

"I tried to open the shed when I burned my hand. I ran to the pond. Stuck my hand in. Slipped and fell in. Got out of the pond. Ran for help. Saw you driving by and led you back to the shed."

"Good. Again."

We rehearsed it seven or eight more times before

we made it to the hospital. Mr. Antenelli carried Bruce through the front doors. *It must be an odd scene*, I thought. This white man bringing in another injured black kid through their doors.

A nurse who was passing by saw Bruce and immediately took him back through the doors. I took a seat in the waiting room, cold and wet.

Mr. Antenelli came back out and told me to come back.

"Listen, son, only give the information that they ask for. You fell in a pond. If they ask you more, give them more. Understand?"

"Yes sir."

When I went back, I recognized one of the nurses from my last visit.

"Back again so soon?" she asked. I dropped my head and continued to follow Mr. Antenelli.

"Nurse? Here he is. He fell into the pond trying to help his classmate. I think he may have swallowed a bit of water. Can you make sure he's ok? He's also got a nasty burn there on his right hand."

"Yes. Of course. Come with me, young man." She held out her hand to me and I took it. Warm and inviting. I felt tears coming. Why? I couldn't let her see. I wiped them quickly on my sleeve and followed her into the exam room.

"You're quite the little hero. Come, sit down. I want to listen to your lungs. Here," she said pointing to the exam table. I jumped up on the table. She warmed the stethoscope with her breath and lifted my wet shirt. "Oh goodness, you're soaked. Jump down here for a second. Step behind this screen here and take off all your clothes. And put on this gown."

I stepped behind the screen and put on the green gown, trying only to use my left hand. The right one was really starting to hurt now.

"That's backwards, sweetie. Here, slide out of that for a second. I'll look away, sweetie." I slid out of the gown, and she put the gown back on correctly. Back on the table, she warmed the stethoscope again and placed it on my back and asked me to take several deep breaths. "We want to make sure you don't have any water left in your lungs. The man who brought you in mentioned that you had thrown up quite a bit of it already. We just want to be sure. Keep breathing, ok? Deep breaths. Your friend is in rough shape but should be ok."

"He's not my friend," I said before I could think about it.

"Well, even more brave that you would risk your life to save someone you don't even know."

"I know him. He's just not my friend." I couldn't shut up it seemed. I was going to blow this.

"Oh, ok. Well, noble all the same." She moved the bed from a flat position to inclined and asked me to lay down.

"Sweetheart, just to be safe, I'm going to have you breathe this oxygen, ok? Just put this mask on, sit back, relax, and breathe deeply. I've applied some ointment to your hand and I'll wrap it. Looks like you have some second degree burns but nothing to be worried about."

When I woke, I could hear Mr. Antenelli pleading with the doctor. "You know how he is. He's just going to take him home. If it's a matter of payment, I'll pay for it. But you know he needs to stay here overnight just in case. I don't know how long he was in that water. If he dies, do you want that on your conscience?"

"Fine. We'll sign him in as John Doe. If we put his real name in, we will be obligated to call his father. We'll call him in the morning after we're sure he's ok."

"Great. Thank you so much. Could you also give me a call? His father won't take off work to come get him, I can assure you."

"Ok. Fine. I can't know about this. Give your number to the nurse."

"Thanks, Doctor. Really. For everything."

After hearing this, I closed my eyes and drifted off to sleep.

I saw my mother sitting on her haunches on the side of the pond. As I approached her slowly from behind, I could see she had something in her hand. A lily. I slowly sat down next to her, afraid she might take off if I approached too quickly. She looked over and smiled at me warmly.

"Mom? Can you hear me?"

"Of course I can, baby."

"Mom. I miss you so much. Ummm. Are you able to see me, like, all the time?"

At this she just looked at me. There was warmth in her eyes but also deep sadness. She knew what I had done. I can't believe I was still disappointing my mother even after her death. She started to slowly pull the petals off the lily.

"I'm so sorry, Mom. I just couldn't take it anymore."

"Imari, baby. Remember what I told you so many years ago right here on the side of this pond? There's nothing that you could ever tell me that would make me stop loving you."

Smiling at this memory, I said, "Thanks, Mom. I really needed to hear that."

She had finished pulling the last petal off the lily. She stood and dusted the grass off of her white sundress.

"I have to go now, baby."

"Will I still see you in my dreams?"

"Oh, yes. It won't be as much as time passes but when you least expect it, I'll be there. It will just be my way of saying how much I still love you, baby. Always and forever."

I got up to hug her. As I did, I was engulfed in

*such warmness—a bright glowing love that pene-
trated every fiber, every cell, until I was filled with
light and love.*

22

IMARI

When I awoke, I wasn't entirely sure where I was but was quickly reminded when I heard the busy noise of the ER and the beeping of the monitors and felt the stinging from my bandaged hand. The nurse came in and checked my vitals and brought me some breakfast, which I devoured in seconds. Soon, the doctor came into the room and picked up the chart hanging on the edge of my bed.

"You've had quite the eventful few weeks, Imari." Though he'd said it as a statement, I got the sense that he wanted me to respond.

"Yes sir."

"Well, I think you're out of the woods, so let's get you home. Who do you want us to call to come get you?"

"Mr. Antenelli, please sir. I'm staying with them. My father is at work and won't come get me."

He seemed pleased by this response and gave me a tap on the shoulder. "Let's make it a while before we see each other again. Ok?"

Smiling, I said, "Yes sir."

A nurse entered the room and busied herself cleaning up and checking some information on the chart hanging from my bed.

"Feeling better today, honey?"

"Yes ma'am," I answered.

"That's good to hear. Up for seeing visitors?"

Andrea! I thought. "Sure." I sat up in the bed to make myself presentable, but I was shocked when I saw who walked through the door to my room.

"Hi Imari," LeDarius said.

"What are you doing here? Here to make fun of me?"

"Oh shit. No. I saw what you did to the last kid who did that," he said, laughing awkwardly. I continued to look at him suspiciously. "I honestly believe he got what was coming to him."

I've seen this before in my dad's spy shows. He's recording me. He's trying to get evidence to discredit me—to prove to the police that I was lying about what happened by the pond. I decided not to answer him.

"Umm. Bruce said that you tried to set him on fire. That true?"

"What are you doing here?"

"Oh, yeah. We don't have to talk about that man. I guess I just wanted to see how you were doing. This is all just so crazy."

"Which part? The part where you both bullied me for months? Or when you jumped me after school? Or made that horrible picture of my mom?"

LeDarius hung his head in contrition. "When you say it all together like that, it does sound bad. I just thought we just playing around at first. Think things just got out of hand."

"Ok," I said, softening only a little.

With that, he looked up and smiled. "When do you get out of here?" he asked, seemingly relieved of his burden.

At this, the nurse stepped in and said, "Now, actually." Had she been listening in to our conversation? "Let's get you out of here."

I said goodbye to LeDarius and got dressed. At some point in the night, someone had brought me new clothes and shoes. Mr. Antenelli most likely. When he arrived, he signed a few hospital forms and ushered me out to the car.

"Son. How are you feeling? Have you had anything to eat?"

"Yes sir. I had breakfast already. I feel ok."

"Good, good. Look, I've already told the family what happened. Imari, it's important that you stick to the story, understand? You may want to tell Andrea because you're such close friends, but you can't, ever. Understand me?"

"Yes sir."

"I have reported what happened to the police. His father had a few choice words apparently. Too disgusting to repeat. Bruce is still in the hospital. He has a few burns on his arms and suffered from some smoke inhalation but he'll be fine. He's only twelve, so he's likely going to a youth detention center. He, of course, tried to tell his version of what happened. But because of his suspension from school and his attacks on you, no one really believed him. I don't even think his own father does."

I nodded, taking all this in.

"You won't have to go testify in a court, but you will have to give your account to the police. Think you can do that?"

I considered this for a brief moment. "Yes sir. I can."

When we arrived at the Antenellis', Andrea ran out and launched into my arms.

"Imari! I'm so glad you're ok."

"Andrea. Be careful, honey," Mr. Antenelli said, smiling.

"Oh my god. Dad told us what happened. Is your hand ok? What a jerk! I hope he goes to jail for what he did."

"Well, not jail, honey. A youth detention center."

"Whatever. He won't be around here anymore and that's all that matters. Come, Imari, tell me everything."

"Honey. We talked about this. Imari has been through a lot already and we need to be respectful and not force him to be retraumatized by asking him to repeat what happened. You already know. That should be enough."

Rolling her eyes. "Ok, Daddy."

After we finished dinner that evening, Mrs. Antenelli asked, "Do you want to go to school tomorrow, Imari? I don't imagine people at school know yet but it's a small town and everyone seems to know everything. It's up to you, sweetheart."

"Well, honey, I need to take Imari down to the police station in the morning, but Imari, if you want, I can drop you off to school after that."

"Yes sir. That's fine."

That morning, we had breakfast like we had for many weeks now. It seemed so unfair that I would have to say goodbye again to the Antenellis. I felt like I was always saying goodbye to someone lately. I wanted to try and enjoy what might be one of my last meals with the Antenellis but I was too nervous about what was coming up for me this morning. What if the cops saw right through my lie and I was the one that would end up in YDC? I went over the story again and again in my head. I tried to think about what questions the police might ask—something that could trip me up.

"Imari? Did you hear me?" Mrs. Antenelli asked.

I must have been too deep in thought because I had no idea what she had said to me. "No, ma'am. I'm sorry."

"That's ok, sweetheart. I was just asking if you were nervous about having to speak to the police today."

"Oh. Yes ma'am. A little."

"You have nothing to worry about, ok?" With this, she reached over and placed her hand on top of my forearm. "Just tell the truth and everything will be fine. You did nothing wrong."

Seeing my discomfort, Mr. Antenelli interjected. "Imari, son, go brush your teeth and grab your things."

Happy to have an excuse to leave the table, I jumped up quickly from my seat and made a beeline to the bathroom to brush my teeth. I stood in front of the bathroom mirror and, for the first time in a long time, I took a real long look at myself in the mirror. I could hardly recognize the person staring back at me.

Negative thoughts started to enter my head and I broke my gaze with the mirror shaking my head. I needed to stay focused. My life depended on what happened in the next hour. If I went to YDC, I would forever be labeled as a "bad kid." Labels like that are hard to overcome—especially in a small town.

Mr. Antenelli led me into the police station and went up to the front desk.

"You stay here for a second."

"Yes sir."

The station was fairly quiet for a Thursday morning. Maybe it was always this quiet. There was a very distinct odor—old wood, cigarettes, coffee, and sweat. I looked around the station, trying to take in my surroundings, but it just made me more nervous.

"Mr. Antenelli? Hi. I'm Officer Rallings," he said, extending his hand.

"Nice to meet you."

"You two can follow me."

I'd seen many police shows. My dad loved them. I was waiting to be taken to a cold room with no windows, a metal table between me and the officer. Instead, he led us to a desk that sat in a room of desks. There were other officers around having conversations and drinking coffee. None of them even seemed to register me as I walked by. A few, however, gave a quick head nod to Mr. Antenelli.

"Please, have a seat. This won't take long. So, you're, umm, E-mar-e."

"Imari. Yes sir."

The officer seemed pleased when I called him sir.

"Imari. Got it. So, Imari, tell me what happened. This occurred on Tuesday, October 15th. Correct? Between five and six o'clock?"

"Yes sir."

"You had just gotten home a few minutes before five?"

"Yes sir. I had just come from getting my stitches out."

"Stitches he needed because he was attacked by Bruce in the very shed where he tried to set up a trap for Imari," Mr. Antenelli said, eager to participate in the discussion.

"Thank you, Mr. Antenelli, but I really need this statement to be in Imari's own words."

Mr. Antenelli put both hands up and gave a slight nod before sliding back in his seat.

"Now, Imari. Tell me what you did when you got home from school."

"I like to go to a pond and sit. It's where me and my mom used to go a lot."

"Right. Yes. I read that you just lost your mom. I'm sure that must be hard." I nodded my head. "Keep going."

"I saw smoke coming from the old shed in the distance and then it caught fire. Then I heard screaming."

"Now, how far would you say you were from the shed when you heard the screaming."

"It's about fifty yards," Mr. Antenelli said not able

to stop himself. Officer Rallings cut his eye sharply at Mr. Antenelli. "Sorry, sorry."

"Fifty yards. Does that sound right, Imari?"

"Yes sir."

"Ok. Then what happened?"

"I ran up to the shack and tried to get in."

"And was it hard to get in? How did you try to get in?"

"Well," I said, giving it some thought. I hadn't really thought about it in this level of detail. "I tried opening the door to the shed. It wasn't too hard but as soon as I opened the door, there was smoke everywhere. I stepped in with both hands out and my right hand started to sting so bad that I had to turn around."

"What caused it to sting?"

"I wasn't sure then but now I know it was fire. I just knew I had to get out of there and put my hand in water to stop the stinging." Officer Rallings nodded. "When I went to put my hand in the pond, I fell into the pond."

"And how long do you think you were in the pond?"

"I don't know."

"Ok. What next?"

"I got out of the pond and went to run for help."

"Did you look back to see if the shed was still on fire?"

"I think so." I paused to see if Officer Rallings had

any follow up questions before I continued. "When I made it to the street, Mr. Antenelli was just driving by. So, I stopped him and took him to the shack, and he saved Bruce."

"Ok. Thanks, Imari. Now, Mr. Antenelli. Roughly what time was this that Imari stopped you on the street?"

"It would have been between 5:20 p.m. and 5:30 p.m. I had left work around 5:00 p.m."

"And someone at your job can corroborate this?"

"I'm sure someone could. There were other people in the office." Eager to move this along, Mr. Antenelli continued unprompted. "So, I get to the shed, go inside, and pull Bruce out."

"And where was Bruce?"

"He was stuck in some hole he'd dug. Likely some trap he had for Imari."

"Why do you think it was a trap?"

"Officer, you already know what happened in that same shed a few weeks ago. This boy has terrorized Imari for years and it has just continued to escalate this school year. I know the boy doesn't have the best home life. I even tried to have civil conversations with Bruce's father, but he just told me to 'stay out of black folks' business.'"

"When did you try talking to his father?"

"It was weeks ago."

"Ok. So, you take both boys to the hospital. Records from the hospital show that that was just before 6:00 p.m. Is that right?"

"I think so, yes."

"Right," Officer Rallings said as he slid back in his squeaky chair—reclining as he put both hands behind his head. "Of course, Bruce has a different story. He says that Imari set this trap for him."

"Please! Of course that's what he's going to say. Imari has never fought back against Bruce and there are many people—students, teachers, parents—who would testify to that. Bruce is a troubled child and a bully and he needs help and that father of his certainly isn't going to do anything."

I waited. My palms were sweating. I knew more questions were coming. He knew something he wasn't telling us. There was some piece of evidence left at the scene. That's how it always happened in the shows my dad watched. Officer Rallings sat up in his chair and closed the notebook where he had been taking notes and looked at me.

"Imari, do you have anything else you want to tell me?"

Oh god, I thought. *This is it. He knows.* Panicking, I looked down at the ground, too afraid to look at Mr. Antenelli. Finally, I was able to say in a bit of a whisper, "No sir."

"Fine. Ok. Thanks both of you for coming in. If I have any more questions, I'll give you a call."

We both got up quickly and left the station. In the

car, we both took a huge sigh of relief. Had I been holding my breath that entire time? Mr. Antenelli patted me on the shoulder and said, "You did good, son."

I looked over at him—sun gleaming through the window of the car—and smiled at him. This man had done so much for me—more than my own father ever would have done. In that moment, I felt lucky to have the Antenellis in my life. I was going to be devastated when I eventually had to go back home again.

23

IMARI

Weeks passed. As Mrs. Antenelli had predicted, rumors had started to fly around the school about what happened in the shed. Bruce had indeed been sentenced to two years in YDC. He would never go back to school again. Of course, people had asked me what happened, but I wouldn't talk about it. If Andrea or I was in earshot of teachers, they would stop the conversations altogether. One of the more outrageous rumors I'd heard was that Bruce had tied me up naked and was trying to roast me over a fire.

I was still staying with the Antenellis and I wasn't complaining about it. I would occasionally see my father coming home from work, but he mostly never even acknowledged me except for one day in the spring. It was a Saturday and the last bit of frost from winter had been melted away and the grass was starting to grow again. I was walking by the house when my father stopped me.

"Hey boy. You been in my shit?"

I guess I knew he might ask me this at some point, but I certainly had no plans on telling him the truth.

"No."

"No? No what, boy? You start living with those white people and you think you're better than me? I'm still your father."

At this, I rolled my eyes and started to walk away.

"Hey boy. Get back here. I'm not done talking to you. Where my gas can? And did you take some of my wood?"

I could see him starting to piece things together. I needed this conversation to end and quickly, but it was too late.

"Well, well. I didn't know you had it in you. Not a punk after all."

I knew that my father meant this as some sort of compliment, but it made me sick to my stomach. I just turned and walked away. I couldn't identify the feeling I had in the pit of my stomach. Was I worried he would tell the police? When I thought about it, I knew the answer was no. Despite how disappointed he was in what sort of son I was, he would never voluntarily have a conversation with the police.

Mr. Antenelli saw me walking up the hill, deep in thought. He called out to me to come assist him with something. He was showing me the plans he had for the downstairs. The drawings he was showing me didn't make any sense to me and I was still distracted by my conversation with my dad.

"Imari, son, are you doing ok?"

I blurted out, "My dad knows."

"Knows what?"

"Knows what I did to Bruce."

At this, Mr. Antenelli moved closer and knelt down to be on my level and whispered, "How do you know?"

"He went to cut grass and saw that his gas can was missing and some wood."

"Shit. Sorry," Mr. Antenelli said—apologizing for his language. "Do you think he's going to say anything?"

"No. He won't. I actually think he was proud of me."

Relieved, Mr. Antenelli sat on the floor and crossed his legs, leaning back on his hands. There had been something that had been bothering me about that day and now felt like the time to ask.

"Mr. Antenelli. What really happened that day? How did you know to come looking for me?"

Mr. Antenelli got very serious and considered this for a moment before saying, "Imari, we're going to talk about this now and then we're never going to talk about this again. Understood?"

"Yes sir."

He began to organize his thoughts. "Here's the thing, Imari. I knew you were up to something. A few times, I actually followed you out to the pond to check on you. I was worried that you might do something to yourself. Then, I was hoping you were just being a boy and building something in the shed. When you weren't there, I went in and saw that you were digging a hole and that you had gathered some rocks and were mixing some sort of mud. Even then I thought—maybe this is going to be some sort of fire pit. So, I had started pulling my car off into an alley around the corner each day on the way home from work and checking in to see what was going on. On that day, when I started to make my way through the trail, I could smell the smoke and I could hear screaming. When I got to the pond and saw you, I was relieved until I realized that I could still hear screaming. After I had pulled Bruce from the fire, you were nowhere to be found. I thought maybe you had gotten scared and ran away. But when I walked by the pond with Bruce in my arms, I could see bubbles coming up from the pond and I jumped in to save you." He stopped to allow a few moments for this all to sink in.

As the scene formed in my head, a question started to surface. "What about your clothes?"

"My clothes?"

"Yes. Wouldn't they have been wet from jumping in the pond to save me?"

"That's some great analytical thinking, Imari. Maybe you should be an engineer," he said, drifting off topic. "You know, it never came up. No one seemed to notice that my clothes were wet or that I changed into my gym clothes once you were back with the doctor, and I had called Mary."

"And what about Mrs. Antenelli? Does she know the truth? Did she wonder why you were in your gym clothes when you came home?"

"Well, she was in the kitchen when I got home and I quickly showered and picked up some dry, clean clothes to bring back to the hospital for you. It was a hard decision I had to make in the moment—to tell a lie and to keep that lie from my wife. I felt like it was the best thing to do at the time to make sure you were safe and didn't get into trouble. Maybe if I had it to do over again, I might tell Mary everything. She was just so worried. She wanted to come back with me to the hospital, but we decided it was probably best if she stayed home in case your father showed up and made trouble."

This settled the questions I had about that day and I was ready to put that day behind me but Mr. Antenelli had one more thing he needed to discuss about that day before closing the topic.

"Imari, you have to promise me something, ok?"

"Yes sir."

"If you ever again feel like you want to hurt yourself, will you tell me first?"

"Ok. I will."

GEORGE

Every day bleeds into the next now. So much paper-work to sign, things to go through and get rid of. My Imani was a simple woman so there wasn't much to box up. While going through old boxes, I had found some keepsakes—birthday cards, old photos, a menu from the diner where we had our first date. I couldn't cry anymore. Maybe it was the alcohol or shock. Hell if I know. All I know is that I needed all reminders of that old life gone. It was just a constant reminder of what a horrible husband I had been and what a failure I had been as a father. I would sign over my parental rights. He was never really my son. I never could show up for him in the way that Imani wanted me to. Maybe I resented him for trapping me in this life or maybe it was as Imani had laid out to me in her letter. Her letter. While I had skimmed through it in the attorney's office to make sure it was legit, I hadn't read it through start to finish. It was the last thing I needed to do to finally let her go. I sat down at the kitchen table—where she and the boy had spent so much time together—and slid the letter carefully out of the envelope. The envelope was wavy to the touch in some places—some spots. Had I cried in that attorney's office when he handed it to me? It all seems like many lifetimes ago now.

I opened the letter and began to read.

> *My Dearest George,*
>
> *Sweetheart, I know this will be difficult for you to read and if you are reading this, then the worst has happened. God only knows what you're going through right now and how you're dealing with this. I don't mean to add to this difficult time. Quite the opposite really. There are some things I need to say and some last wishes I need you to do for me.*
>
> *First, I hope you know how much I loved you. And even though you'd long lost the ability to show it to me in return, I know you loved me too. I only wished things could have been different—that you would have allowed yourself to really show up and receive the love I was giving you and that your son would have given you if you showed any interest in him at all. He deserves to have a good life and we both know that he can't get that with you. You know I've never asked you for much, but this is a big one and I need you to just do it without making this hard for anyone involved. I've asked the Antenellis to raise Imari. They already think of him as a part of their family and he and Andrea are already the best of friends. It would be nice if he could have been raised by someone in my own family, but we don't get to choose the family we're born into. Mine wanted nothing to do with me,*

so I refuse to let them have anything to do with my son. The lawyer has assured me that as long as you don't protest, my family will have no legal right to my son. And I say my son, because that's who he always was.

Second, I wish to be cremated. I have already left instructions at the funeral home and have put their business card here in the envelope with who you should contact when I'm gone. I know how you felt about cremation but as I sit here writing this, I am a shell of myself. I don't want to be remembered that way.

Finally, I want you to try to be happy. Remarry if you want. Try again at having a family. I know that person I met so many years ago, the guy I made out with passionately under that lamppost, is still in there. Don't waste the rest of your life feeling sorry for not loving me the way you should have or for giving up your son. Take it from me, life is too short to waste time regretting what could have been.

I'll love you always.
Imani

I took a deep breath and closed my eyes—folded the letter and put it back in the envelope. There was only one of her wishes that I could fulfill. I would give up Imari to the Antenellis. Imani was right. We would both be miserable if I didn't. He had a right to get some joy in his life—to have a father who really loved him and that wasn't me. I couldn't cremate her though. I just couldn't bring myself to do it. And I would never marry again. There was too much darkness in my soul to even conceive of love. No. The world would be much better if I kept all this darkness to myself.

24

MARY

Many weeks had passed now since the horrible fall we had last year. It took us months to sort out things with George, but we were finally at the last step and ready to talk to Andrea and Imari about the adoption. Imari would be our son officially. We wanted to make sure we were doing the best for everyone involved. Imani's family had tried to make a claim on Imari but Imani had been very clear about her wishes. In the end, that's what made the process move so smoothly. George had shown up many times drunk if he'd shown up at all. The court-appointed mediator had certainly made note of it. He was clearly in no shape to provide a stable home environment for Imari. And while he did protest a little at the beginning, his heart wasn't really in it. His car was in his driveway most days. Andrew thought he'd likely been fired from his job. Imani did mention to me that George had taken out a life insurance policy on each of them when they were first married. It wasn't enough for him to live on for very long but that probably explained it. By the beginning of the summer, George had signed over his parental rights, which cleared the way for our adoption.

Now, we wanted to have a chat with Andrea. To bring another child into your home, it's not something to be taken lightly. I had heard all of the horror stories—mostly from my mother. I didn't want Andrea to feel like her opinion didn't matter. We knew that she loved Imari but maybe she would feel differently about him actually being her brother. Andrew and I sat down with her alone one day while Imari was meeting with a therapist. Andrea had come with us to drop Imari off and we had gone to the park.

"Mom, can I go play on the swings?" Andrea had asked.

"Before you do, your father and I need to talk to you."

"What did I do now?"

"It's not anything like that at all, sweetheart. Sit down here at this picnic table."

Andrea sat down at the table, looking up at us with a cross between concern and impatience.

"Honey, how have you liked having Imari live with us?"

"Oh no! You're not sending him back to live with his father! Mom, Dad, you can't!"

"No Andrea. We are not," Andrew interjected. "It's quite the opposite. We wanted to know how you'd feel about Imari living with us permanently."

"That would be great! I know Imari would love that. He hasn't said it to me but I can tell he's worried about when he has to go back home. But what about his dad? Will he be ok with it?"

"Well, honey, you know that me and Imari's mom got very close in the weeks before she passed away."

"Yes."

"She asked me, us really, that if anything ever happened to her if we would raise Imari as our own child."

At this Andrea's eyes lit up. "So, he'd be my brother?"

"Yes," I said.

"Wow. That's amazing, Mom and Dad."

"So, you're happy about this?" Andrew asked.

"Over the moon!"

"That's so great to hear, honey. We just want you to know that we love you very much. Imari needs a lot of our attention right now to help him through everything that he's dealing with but please know that we are here for you too. If you're ever starting to feel like you need more from us, you can just talk to us, ok?"

"Yes, Mom. I understand. Does Imari know? Can I tell him?"

"He doesn't know yet. So you can't tell him. Your Mom and I are going to talk to him about it tonight. So please, not a word about it."

"Ok, Dad."

IMARI

The rest of the school year went by in a flash and summer was upon us. Andrea was hanging out more with Angie and I had started to make my own friends at school and a couple of friends in the neighborhood. I was still waiting for the moment when I'd have to pack my things up and move back home. I didn't want to go back so I certainly wasn't going to bring it up. But then, one day in mid-July, Mr. and Mrs. Antenelli sat me down at the dining room table for a chat. *This is it,* I thought. *I'm going back home.*

I could never have foreseen what happened next.

"Imari, sweetheart. We wanted to talk to you for a moment. Andrew and I have loved having you stay here with us. You've become a part of our family." Mrs. Antenelli paused and took Mr. Antenelli's hand. "You're like a son to us. We've talked with your dad. He just hasn't really dealt well with losing your mom and he doesn't really feel like he can take care of you. So, and sweetheart, this is only if this is what you want, we want to know if you'd like to live here with us—for good."

I blurted out, "Yes! I'd love to live here. Thank you."

Mr. Antenelli joined in the conversation.

"Imari, you wouldn't just live here. Your father has agreed to release his parental rights to you. We'd adopt you. You'd be our son."

I looked back and forth between the Antenellis. I didn't even know that this was a thing people could do. Suddenly, I started to think about my mom. What would she think?

Seeming to sense this, Mrs. Antenelli added, "Another thing, Imari. When I was sitting with your mom during one of her chemo sessions, she asked me if we would take care of you. It was a really difficult thing for her to ask us to do but she really did believe that it was the best option. And you wouldn't have to call us Mom and Dad. I will never take your Mom's place, Imari. You can come up with whatever makes you feel comfortable. But we would have to change your last name. You'd no longer be a Johnson. You'd be Imari Antenelli."

"Imari Antenelli," I said, trying it on for size and smiling.

"So, what do you think, son?"

I could see the anticipation in their eyes.

I got up from the seat and ran into their arms.

On July 21, 1987, I became Imari Antenelli at the courthouse in a very short court proceeding. Afterwards, we all went out for pizza and cake and celebrated the day. In many ways, it was like a birthday. I was now an Antenelli and would be for the rest of my life.

When we returned from the restaurant, I asked if I could go to the pond alone. I had only been back there a handful of times since the incident with Bruce. The lilies were in full bloom now and I could smell their scent as soon as I stepped out from the trail. The ducks were back, and they seemed happy to see me. I had kept a few of the breadsticks from dinner so I could feed them. I tried to keep my eyes focused on the pond, but I couldn't resist looking up at the old shed. I was shocked by what I saw. I got up from the pond and made my way over to where the shed had once stood but there was no evidence that a shed was ever there. I would find out later that Mr. Antenelli had spoken with the owner of the land and asked if he could take it down. In its place, Mr. Antenelli had seeded the ground with grass seed and had transferred a few of the lilies from around the pond along with some other wildflowers. Over time, this spot would be indistinguishable from the surrounding land—except for the lilies.

25

TWENTY YEARS LATER

IMARI

The flight from California was a long one with two young kids in tow. My wife Emily carried the brunt of the responsibility with our newborn daughter, Imani. We'd agreed very early on before we were even married that we would name our first-born daughter after my mother and our first-born son after her father, Jack. It was Imani's first flight, and we were very nervous how she'd handle the change in air pressure on the five-hour flight. It was Emily's idea to make little goodie bags for the rest of the first-class passengers, apologizing in advance for any crying or wailing. The bags went over well with a lot of the female passengers stopping by to say hello.

Once on the ground and in the rental car, we made the hour and a half trip back to the old neighborhood. We had been back a few times with Jack—usually for Thanksgiving. This would be the first time in years where we would all be back home together—all the kids. Andrea worked for several non-profits around the globe, providing legal assistance to underserved populations. She was currently working with an organization in Tupelo, Mississippi and en route home as well for a few days. Jeffrey was in his junior year at Georgia Tech, studying electrical engineering. It was spring break, so he was going to drive up to meet his niece for the first time.

When we pulled up, Ma was standing at the doorway in her apron—no doubt cooking and baking for days leading up to our arrival.

"Jack, look! It's MiMi. Go say hello."

I released Jack from his car seat. He was nearly at the age where he wouldn't need it anymore. Ma leaned down and wrapped her arms around Jack who relaxed into her embrace.

"Hi, Ma," I said giving her a hug and kiss on the cheek. "I hope you haven't been cooking all day."

"Well, of course I have been! And I made your favorite!"

"Your mac and cheese? Mmmm. I can't wait!"

"Oh, and who is this?" Ma said as her voice seemed to raise a few octaves. "Oh my god, give me that baby! Hi Emily, sweetheart. How was the flight?" Ma took Imani from my wife and immediately smelled the crown of her head. "That smell. It's magical."

"Ma? Is Dad downstairs?"

"Yes. Yes. Fiddling with something or other. Why don't you go down and help him? I think he said there was something wrong with a router or something? I don't know."

Ma turned and continued talking to Imani and showing her around the kitchen.

"Jack, you come with me."

Downstairs there was my dad cursing under his breath as he tried to trace the wires from the back of the modem. I stood there for a moment, just watching him and smiling. This man was my father. My biological father had died years ago from cirrhosis of the liver and the home I grew up in sat vacant. The home apparently was tied up in probate as my father had no living next of kin. My mother's name was never on the deed to the house. I decided early on that I would call Mr. Antenelli Dad, and Mrs. Antenelli Ma. Mom was reserved for my amazing mother Imani. Mrs. Antenelli, of course, understood.

"Dad! Now, you watch your language. We don't want Jack repeating any of that filth coming out of your mouth," I said, struggling to keep a straight face.

Dad got up from the floor and dusted off his pants, laughing.

"Jack, you see how your father talks to his ol' man?"

Jack looked up at me, giggling. Dad moved in and grabbed me by the back of my neck and pulled me into a hug.

"Good to see you, son. Now, help me fix this thing. Our internet just stopped working this morning. Your mother was down here vacuuming earlier. I don't know if we shorted something out or what."

I looked over where the modem was and there were no lights showing. I could see that it was plugged into the wall but not quite all the way. I pushed the plug into the wall outlet completely and the lights on the modem started blinking.

"Oh, you think you're so smart!" Dad said as he gave me a slight push.

"Happy to help. That'll be $100."

"Add it to my tab."

Dad showed me and Jack all the projects he was working on around the house in various stages of progress. Jack seemed very interested in all the woodwork and immediately wanted to play with the most dangerous tools.

"Dad, let's go up so you can meet your granddaughter."

"Another woman who's gonna have me wrapped around her finger, no doubt."

A few hours later, after catching up with my folks,

I took Jack for a walk down the hill.

"Honey, we'll be back in a little bit. I wanna show Jack the old pond."

"Son, you know there's a house there now where the trail used to be. You'll have ask the Montgomerys if you can cut through their backyard."

"Ok, Dad. Come on, Jack. Let's go for a walk."

As we made our way down the hill, I started to point things out to Jack. This is the tree I used to love to climb. Here is where my mom taught me how to ride a bike. And here is the house where I grew up. Standing there looking at the house with its over-grown weeds and loose shutters and peeling paint, memories started flooding back to me. We walked up the driveway, confident that there was no one living in the house. There, under a tarp that was heavy-leaden with pollen and pine needles, was our old white truck, the Voyageur.

"Son, this is the truck I was telling you about. My mom used to sit up front and I would sit in the truck bed. She'd slide open the back window and ask me where I wanted to go—so many adventures we had in this truck."

"It's old and dirty, Dad."

"Yes, son. But use your imagination. You've seen pictures of your grandma. Imagine her here in this truck and me as a kid right around your age in the back. Now, of course, they don't let you do that these days but, back then, riding in the back of a truck felt like riding a steed into battle."

I looked down at Jack and I could see his little mind trying to form the picture and a smile came to my face. Would he remember this moment like I still remember all the wonderful moments with my mom?

Mr. Montgomery had come outside now and was watching us from his front porch. I waved at him, and he waved back as we walked towards him.

"Hi there. How's it going?"

"Fine. Fine. You related to the man who used to live here?"

I considered this for a moment. Technically, the man who died in this house was not my father and we were not related anymore.

"I grew up in that house," I said. It seemed to be the best way to respond. "Do you know if there's a way to the old pond that is back behind your house?"

"Hmm. I'm not sure. I can't get my own kids to play outside. You know how kids are these days. Anyway, I've never been back there myself so I'm not sure. You're welcome to have a look. There's a door at the back of the gate. Enjoy your adventure," Mr. Montgomery said, directing that at Jack.

He looked up at me—eyes filled with excitement.

When we stepped through the gate, I surveyed the landscape. Nothing really looked familiar. I tried to imagine where the old path started back at the street and where we would need to go to connect back up to it from where we were. I could see the worry in Jack's face as he saw the overgrown woods in front of us. I picked him up in my arms and carried him as I searched for a good entry point.

After a few moments of testing different paths, I found one that looked promising and stepped inside over some downed branches. I had found it! The old path. Then, my memory took over from all the times I had walked this path in my youth. It was overgrown for sure, but I could still make it out. When we exited the woods, there it was—as beautiful as I had remembered it. I put Jack down and we walked towards the pond. There were no ducks here today. Maybe they had stopped coming when I left for college. They always seemed to know when to show up.

"Jack. Stay here for just a moment. I'll be right back." I could see worry in his face. "I'm just going right over there. You'll still be able to see me."

I searched for the place where the old shed was, but this was much harder to remember. The landscape was overgrown with wildflowers. Just as I was about to give up, I saw them just off in the distance. The lilies that my dad had planted long ago when he took down the shed. I walked around the area looking for any signs of the shed when a flicker of light caught my eye. There, buried under some of the tall grass, was something that looked like a piece of glass. I reached down to investigate and immediately recognized it. It was my old Casio watch! God. It must have slid off my wrist that day.

I grabbed the watch and took it over to show Jack.

Back at the pond, I knelt behind Jack as my mother had done many, many years ago. There was a slight breeze causing ripples on the water and there were a few birds in the distance, deep in conversation. It was up to me now to carry on the tradition of creating magic and wonder with my words. I took a breath and said to Jack, "Son, I want to tell you a story."

AUTHOR'S NOTE

When I sat down at my computer almost a year ago, it was with a simple idea to write a short story about a boy who was ruthlessly bullied to the point where he had no choice but to fight back. It was a story that I knew well having endured years of bullying myself as a child.

In my own story, there were friends who refused to leave my side even as the bullying reached the point where I refused to leave the house during the summers. I have vivid memories of being secluded in my bedroom and hearing the kids in my neighborhood just outside my window laughing and playing. I desperately wanted to join them.

It was likely because of those many hours alone in my room, that I learned how to foster my imagination

—creating characters in my head to be my friends, worlds where I could be the hero and triumph over my imagined evils.

To all who may read this book, I hope that you see how absolutely essential it is for those of us who might endure oppression to have those who are willing to stand with us—who are willing to face persecution when it would be just as easy to walk away. For me, those people were Shania and Curtis. To each of you, I say, "Thank you!" You showed me what it meant to be a real friend and gave me hope in humanity. You'll never know how much your friendship meant to me.

Finally, while I grew up in North Georgia and was bullied as a kid, this story is not autobiographical. However, like any new writer, I have written from what I know so there are of course experiences in this novel that are like situations I experienced myself around the same age as Imari. But this is a work of fiction and one that I am very proud of.

— T.S. Riley

Milton Keynes UK
Ingram Content Group UK Ltd.
UKHW021836130624
444169UK00001B/33